More Than Words

♡

KARLA DOYLE

COPYRIGHT

To Todd and Amanda, for nagging me daily to get off Twitter and finish writing the damn book.

I love you guys so much!

For Lisa C. You kept me F&P every time my writerly ADD threatened to sneak in. Your praise, honest criticism and chat-room floggings kept me on track.

So glad we found each other, my friend.

And always, a special thank you to Grace Bradley, my incredible editor. Not a day goes by that I don't thank my lucky stars to have snagged you.

Table of Contents

Chapter One

The soft music ended mid-song, replaced by a throbbing dance mix.

Calli glanced at her watch. Five on the dot. She'd gone to the back office when things died down half an hour ago. By the volume and singing coming from the front of the store, Caitlyn had already flipped the sign and locked the door. Calli followed the techno beat and found Caitlyn's backside in clubbing mode, swaying and thrusting to the music as she refolded panties at light speed.

Excited about going out... must be nice.

"I'll do that, you're off the clock," Calli said, pulling a tiny pink thong from her sister's manicured hands.

"Hey, boss lady. Checked the till—another totally awesome day today. A thirty-percent increase over this day last year."

Despite being relieved of duty, Caitlyn continued stacking underwear into organized piles. Every time the song's chorus came on, she gave Calli a hip bump. Caitlyn was a force of nature, impossible to resist, and Calli found herself bumping alongside her before the song changed. Smiling, even.

Finished with the bottoms, they moved to the wall displays and began straightening bras, peignoir sets, nighties and robes. Calli had lucked out hiring her little sister. Caitlyn had the looks of a gorgeous plus-size model, the sex appeal of a centerfold and the dedication of a business partner—even though she wasn't one. Customers loved her. Calli loved her. And by the never-ending pings and chimes coming from Caitlyn's cell phone in her pocket, plenty of other people loved her. And were waiting.

"Get out of here, now. That's an order."

"Okay, I'm going." Caitlyn practically bounced across the room with her purse and jacket. "You should come with us. There are soooo many hot guys there."

"Sounds great. I'll pass."

"You have something against hot guys?"

"You know I don't." Calli turned away from her sister and continued straightening racks. Celibacy sucked. The toys she sold at Romance U were a sorry substitution for a flesh-and-blood partner. She'd happily trade their ability to go all night for a hit of hot manliness. If only it were that easy.

A reassuring arm folded around her shoulder. "Hey... I'd be with you the whole time. I promise not to leave you alone, not even for a second."

Late-night clubbing with Caitlyn and her outgoing, fun-loving crew. The music, dancing and laughing would be fun, but it was just... impossible.

"Tell me all about the hot guys tomorrow. Take some pictures on your phone and text them to me."

Caitlyn sighed, her lips drawing downward. "I'll let you off the hook for now, but I'm not giving up on you. Not ever."

"Even if I wasn't the Wikipedia poster girl for fucked-up, I'd still be too busy to go out. It's that time of year." She waved off the incoming pity hug. "I'm fine." Bullshit, and both of them knew it. "Go, have fun."

The store in order a short time later, Calli double-checked the locks, turned out the lights, collected the day's receipts and climbed the back stairs. Dancing of the four-legged variety was happening on the other side of the closed door. She opened it slowly, not wanting to send Prince Charming flying across the room.

"There's my big boy." She bent to scoop up all eight pounds of him. "I missed you too." Bumping and grinding with hot men had nothing on cuddling with a Chihuahua that vibrated faster than the high-speed setting on her bullet. Right. Sure it didn't.

By the time she'd finished with her spreadsheets and supper, the November sky was utter blackness. Her love for this time of year died with the closed sign. Business was fantastic, everything else made her want to curl up in a ball and rock until the sun returned. She shut out the night—and the nightlife of Belmont Village—with each snap of blinds in her little apartment.

She snuggled into the couch with her dog and her laptop. Not much had changed in the blogosphere since her last tea break. She logged into her game center and played all her moves within ten minutes. None of her book club buddies were online to return the favor—even *they* had lives after sundown. Saturday night television sucked. She could read, but her latest batch of romance novels was in a pile by her bed. Too far away.

She drummed her purple nails on the side of the computer. "This takes pathetic and desperate to a new low." She keyed in the address one of her Scrabble pals had forwarded. *Online games for the friendly and the flirtatious*, the website's banner bragged. Ha. Online games for the homely and pathetic was probably closer to the truth. And she was one of them.

She set up a user ID and entered a bunch of profile information. A few clicks later, a list of open games popped up. Lots of animated avatars with big eyes and bigger boobs stared out from the screen. Ugh, lame. A dramatic black rose caught her attention, the perfect counter to her red rose avatar. Travis—male, thirty-two, single, heterosexual, located in Southern Ontario, it read. Heterosexual her ass. Not with a flower as his profile pic. No sexy guys for her, not even in cyberspace.

Whatever Travis might be like in real life, he was an aggressive Scrabble player. Calli respected that. Hell, it was kind of exciting, sad as that was. Halfway through their game he played *quartz* for one hundred forty-five points. She'd been playing Scrabble since the third grade, probably had thousands of games under her belt, but she'd never scored that high with a single word. The move was smokin', whether he was or not.

Her fingers hovered over the keyboard. To chat, or not to chat. Might as well…she was here to be friendly and flirtatious, right? She rolled her eyes at the screen, typed her message in the chat pane and hit the send key with gusto.

You're kicking my ass.

A reply popped up immediately, one that made Calli choke on her root beer.

Want me to kiss it better?

His comment shouldn't have come as a surprise. The site was for playing games of the social kind, not just the wordy kind. Truth was, she'd been hoping for something more exciting than triple-word scores and bingos. Now the dark rose, Travis, was inviting her to play a different kind of game. Her secret extroverted side jumped in.

Maybe. Depends on what type of kisser you are.

His reply came immediately. *One who pays attention to the woman I'm kissing.*

The number of guys Calli had kissed in her thirty-one years could be counted on her hands. None of those men could make that sort of boast. All the kissing she'd experienced belonged in one of three not-so-exciting categories—slobbery, dry as the Sahara, and look-out-here-comes-my-giant-tongue. Her dates had kissed a set of lips, not Calli the woman.

She sighed and hit send. *Then you have a very lucky girlfriend.*

Not currently. What I have are lonely lips. Help me out, pucker up.

Cute. Well, his humor was, anyway. Travis probably had a great personality and mutt-ugly looks, a diamond inside a lump of coal. Otherwise, why would he be hanging out online on a Saturday night? Playing Scrabble, no less. Since they were in cyberspace, though, all that mattered was the diamond part.

She typed in her message. *Nice girls don't kiss on the first game board.*

That wasn't exactly a no. Maybe you're not so nice?

In reality, she was nothing but a nice girl. But this wasn't reality. *You're right. Lay one on me...*

What she expected to see was some silly emoticon with big lips that would make her cringe. She braced for it, ready to end their chat at the first sign of a circular, yellow face.

Not so fast. Before I kiss you, I need to know a couple of things.

Not what she was expecting, but it wasn't a smiley, thank god. *Don't worry, I'm clean. No viruses here. Your hard drive is safe.*

Very witty. I like smart women.

Even if they're trolls?

His answer to that one ought to be interesting. Anything other than a *no* was a load of bull.

I bet you're not.

Ha, he managed to worm his way around that question quite nicely. Putting herself down was so automatic, she almost started typing a list of her flaws. But this was virtually anonymous. Travis didn't know she was a fearful, shy, pasty-faced wallflower. Online, she could be anything she wanted to be, all of the things she dreamed of being. Her true, inner self. No one would ever know.

Yep, she was going with that. *Good save. So, what do you want to know?*

Whatever you're willing to tell. Start with your name. Does C Ya stand for something?

She tapped her fingers next to the mouse. Asking about her user name, huh? Telling him her actual name was risky—for more than the obvious safety reasons. Anything that could lead him to discovering the real, incredibly boring Calli Yates was out of the question.

Didn't mean she couldn't answer his question. *Yes, it stands for something.*

Funny girl. So literal.

She smirked at the screen. *What did you expect? I'm a word nerd.*

My favorite. Nerd girls are hot. Travis's message popped up quickly, as the others had. He must have quick fingers…that could come in handy.

Lord, she really was desperate, fantasizing about a faceless man's fingers. She flicked herself in the forehead and typed a message. *My thighs are hot…from the laptop. Does that count?*

Definitely. What else are you going to tell me, my hot-thighed, nerdy girl?

The possession in his question made her shiver. Even when she'd had boyfriends—fleetingly—they'd never done anything to claim her for their own. Not one time. She'd just been too insignificant. Travis had made her feel better in this stint online than any live, in-the-flesh man had ever done. Pretty pathetic.

So for Travis, she'd pretend to be hot. Even if went against her nature and the truth. *I have very long, dark-brown hair. Fair skin and blue eyes.*

Do you wear glasses?

Because all nerds wore glasses, is that what he thought? She tsked at the screen while hitting Enter. *Only safety glasses.*

Interesting. I'm picturing you as a sexy construction worker of some kind.

He'd never have guessed the truth, that she wore them while drilling tiny pilot holes through stones and other doodads for the jewelry making that satisfied her creative bent. But a female construction worker, really?

Close. At the club where I strip, my most popular routine involves a costume of safety glasses, a tool belt and not much else. She hit send on the enormous lie and giggled.

Nice. Work boots or high heels?

Work boots, for authenticity. But with hot-pink, sparkly laces.

I'd pay to see that.

Not a bad idea. Calli had the usual fare in the accessories area of her store—French-maid outfits, nurse costumes, bunny ears with matching fuzzy tails—but this construction babe thing might grow wings and fly. If she couldn't find a kit in one of her wholesaler's catalogs, she'd take a daytime outing to Home Depot and make one herself. Too bad she didn't have a real man to test it on.

Even virtually, outright lying gave her a pang. She'd learned early on that her face gave everything away. Apparently her tendency toward full disclosure carried over to anonymous online conversations. Wordy she might be, worldly she was not. So she typed the truth and banged the Enter key.

Truth time. I'm not an exotic dancer.

So I'll put my five-dollar bill away, but I'd still like to see your costume.

This was nothing more than fantasy talk from a faceless stranger. So why was her pulse jumping? Because she hadn't been treated to this much flirtation since the ninth grade, when her fully developed thirty-six C cups earned her extra attention for a while, that's why.

This was much more fun.

She hurried to type a comeback. *For all you know, I might be the most hideous woman in the world, with three arms and a giant, hairy mole.*

His reply appeared even quicker. *The extra arm could have its advantages, so I guess it all depends where that mole is. Do tell.*

Her laughter was startling against the silence of her apartment, making Charming jump off the couch, a totally disgruntled expression on his furry face.

Are you as cute as you are funny?

Not really. Still want me to virtually kiss you?

Huh. He could've said yes, she'd never know the truth. Yet he hadn't. Now that was sexy. She typed, *I'm waiting.*

His message took longer to pop up than the previous ones—totally worth the wait. *Your hair feels like silk around my fingers. I could touch it for hours. The back of your neck fits perfectly in my hand. You're soft and warm... your pulse is pounding faster than before.*

Calli's hand moved to her throat. He was right, it was

hammering like crazy.

Another message appeared on his side of the window. **And now you're blushing.**

Her cheeks were on fire—he was right about that too. **Everything makes me blush, it's a curse.**

No way. Blushing makes you irresistible. And that shy smile. Such pretty lips. Soft too. Sweet. Your mouth is smooth and warm. Delicious, like fruit.

Calli's head fell back as she closed her eyes, letting the fantasy wash over her. She touched her lips. They parted slightly, as if the tips of her fingers were his lips, his tongue. It'd been so long since she'd had a real kiss. Even a sloppy one would be better than nothing at this point.

The computer beeped her back to reality. **It's your move.**

Oh God, he was expecting her to reciprocate. This was bad. Very, very bad.

Give me a minute to think of something… Sorry, I'm a cyber-virgin. She slapped both palms over her face. God, how lame was that?

Another ping from the computer and she peeked out between her fingers to read Travis's message. **I meant it's your move in the game, as in Scrabble. But thanks for sharing. It's an honor to be your cyber-first.**

She groaned. **You must be laughing your ass off over there.**

No, but I am smiling. You're fun. Funny too, in a good way.

Well, that made another first. Responsible, mature, shrewd and dependable—those she was used to hearing—never fun or funny. *So are you. Now sit back and get ready for it, because I'm going to rock your world... with my next word.*

Their playful banter ended while they played a series of rapid-fire moves. He was a wicked opponent, demolishing any hope she had of catching him.

A gentleman would ease up and give a girl a chance.

Who said I was a gentleman? I prefer to dominate.

She snorted. *Ballsy guy. I have no intention of resigning.*

Good, I don't want you to quit. Now submitting, that's another story altogether.

A shiver rippled through her at the implications. *Surely you don't expect me to refer to you as Scrabble Master T.*

Drop the Scrabble and the T.

So I should call you Master?

That works for me.

"Works for me too," she said to the screen. Limited as her sexual experiences were, Calli knew one thing without a doubt—she wanted a man who would take charge behind closed doors. An experienced, confident man who would drive her wild with his carnal skills, introduce her to pleasures she'd only dreamed about. Too bad that kind of man would never want her.

What do you really look like, Master? She hit send, sat back and waited for the rock star description to roll in.

Short brown hair, hazel eyes. Giant, hairy mole on my stomach and a third arm growing out of my side.

Calli laughed out loud. Travis's answer was perfect. *Ooh, we match. I like a man who's dangerously hairy and has a nicely positioned third arm.*

Damn. Now I wish I really had that extra arm.

An automated message popped up, declaring Travis the winner. Game over. The end.

Saying congratulations seemed too formal after the chat they'd shared. And goodbye... well, she just didn't want to say that. **You won.**

I did, mainly because you were on the other side of the board.

Come on, I don't suck that much!

Not what I meant and you know it, C, though we can discuss how much sucking you should do another time. Regrettably, I have to go to work.

Calli grabbed a crossword magazine from the floor and fanned herself with it while pecking at the keyboard. *Sure. Thanks for the game.*

I'd like to play with you again.

All the boys say that. Or they had in the sixth grade, when she was the first girl to get breast buds.

I bet they do. Who do they ask for when they call you out to play? Give me a name to put with my memory of our first virtual date.

She got as far as typing it in the window, then backspaced the whole thing. **You're looking at it. C is my first initial and Ya is the beginning of my last name.**

Thanks for nothing. Where are you, and don't say Ontario, I can see that much.

Temptation licked at her fingertips. Travis seemed great online, but she was no fool. *Location is confidential. For all I know you could be a nutcase, prowling the streets with a beaten-up Scrabble board tucked under your third arm.*

His reply popped up instantly. *So you've seen me around.*

This guy was awesome. And he was about to disappear. *Don't you have to get to work?*

I do. I wish I could call in sick and do this all night.

"Oh, me too." Her fingers flew across the keys, not wanting him to go before he read her message. *So do it. Show me how dominant you really are.*

You tempt me, C. Hairy mole and all.

Um, I forgot to mention that I'm mostly toothless. Does that change how you feel about me? She slapped her forehead. How he felt about her? Good lord, she sounded like a cyber-stalker.

But Travis came back with another cute and sexy line. *I've heard stories about what toothless women can do, so, no.*

You're horrible. I like it. Why can't you call in sick? Yes, she was totally fishing for information. Stupid as that was for so many reasons.

Because I'm irreplaceable.

Me too, it's a burden. To her customers and her dog, if nobody else.

If you won't tell me your name, at least tell me what your real job is. Some crumb to tide me over while I'm bored tonight.

Calli took a minute to think. A little information, nothing too specific, couldn't hurt. And maybe Travis would give something in return.

Truth—I work in a romance store.

A romance store. What does it sell—flowers, lingerie, sex toys?

Pride in her business beat out her need to be secretive. *The works. Something romantic for everyone, for every time. That's the tagline.*

So you're perfect. A woman who likes both Scrabble and sex toys.

Perfect, her? Only in this corner of the internet. *Such assumptions. I only said I work there, not that I like the products.*

And here I thought we were the ideal couple.

"Sure, if you're a neurotic introvert like me," she said to the black rose on her screen. Her fingers said something entirely different. *You tell me what kind of job you're irreplaceable at on a Saturday night and I'll tell you what I really think about sex toys.*

I'm working at a bar. Big one, nothing fancy and no strippers, just rock music and dancing. Now spill.

This secret chat was the most excitement she'd had in... oh, her entire life. Telling intimate truths to a stranger was unbelievably liberating. She started typing, feeling her cheeks lift with a smile her mystery man would never see.

I've tried a few things. All in the name of market research, you know.

For a horribly long minute, nothing new appeared in the chat window. Oh shit, too much information. Way too much. Ten more seconds, then she'd logout and never come back.

I'm going to have a hard time focusing on music tonight. Good thing we'll be playing a lot of covers and I can hide behind my guitar.

"Oh my god, he's a musician." The laptop nearly slid to the floor, her legs were vibrating so much.

Honestly, nothing was sexier than a man playing a guitar. Except maybe a guitar player with kick-ass Scrabble skills and a wonderfully naughty mind who also claimed to be the dominant type. Heaven help her. Full of shit or not, Travis was officially her dream man. Even with his hairy mole and third arm.

Name one song you'll be playing tonight. Then, if I hear it, I'll think of you and feel bad for your, um...preDICKament.

I'm not feeling your sympathy, C. This place is a straight-up rock-and-roll bar. November Rain is an old one, but it's a crowd fave. Know it?

Honestly, was he reading her mind somehow? Did he have visual access to her apartment—a hidden camera that had scoped out her old CD collection on the shelf?

She shook her head while typing. *Of course I know it. I deal in romance.*

I've never heard that song described as romantic.

Then you've been hanging out with the wrong people.

Right on that one. Time to narrow down your

location, Miss Ya-something.

A little narrowing couldn't be all that dangerous, right? *Between Toronto and London. And what makes you think I'm a miss, not a missus... or a mister?*

I read your profile before I accepted the game.

Head, meet desk. If she were at a desk.

Another message from Travis popped up. *Promise me we'll talk again. Soon.*

Could he be asking for more contact than an online Scrabble chat window? No, that was a desperate and ridiculous wish, and one she'd never be able to handle if it materialized in front of her, wrapped in pretty paper with a bow on top. At least he wanted to do *this* again. That was all she needed. Really.

You know how to find me. She rubbed her palms against her pajamas. Too desperate-sounding? Too indifferent? Ugh, this is why she didn't date. Well... one of the lesser reasons, but still. Too stressful.

And I will. Have a great night, C. I'll be thinking about you when we play that song.

Then he was gone. For tonight, at least. Tons of open games waited on the site's homepage, but she wasn't into it anymore. Somewhere out there was a brown-haired guitarist who, in ninety minutes and total anonymity, had made her heart race.

Travis might be that ordinary-looking guy nobody gave a second glance. He might be the ugly guy everybody stares at because they can't look away. Whatever his appearance, she was totally into him. Totally, anonymously into him.

Chapter Two

Eight thirty. Shit, he was late. Travis tossed a handful of kibble in the cat's bowl, grabbed his guitar and jetted out of the apartment. He should have been at The Cove already. The guys were going to have a heyday with this one. Dependable Travis, last one to the gig for once. He could practically hear them now.

He needed something to shut them up. Not the truth. Hell no, if they found out he was late because he met a girl online, and worse, during a Scrabble game—he'd never live it down. Guys who played rock music didn't behave that way. They weren't supposed to behave at all.

The club's parking lot was overflowing when he pulled up. Excellent for his band, even though he had to park down a side street. Not only was Black Box getting the standard flat fee for the gig, they were getting a cut of the bar receipts during, and for an hour after, their set. Thanks to him. The guys never mocked his business savvy. That alone should be enough to keep his bandmates off his back. As if it would.

Fabricating some story was easy enough. The question he couldn't shake was why some faceless female on a geeky game site had gotten to him. Women threw themselves at him all the time—young ones, old ones, and an incredible amount of smoking-hot ones. Even small-time musicians got laid a lot, freely and without any expectation of commitment. A perk of the job, until it grew old. Now he couldn't stop thinking about C Ya, wondering exactly what she looked like, where she lived, if she walked around wearing lingerie just for the hell of being sexy. For all he knew, *she* wasn't even a she. He ought to give his fucking head a shake.

"Cat puked on my clothes," Travis said as he climbed onstage, past a bunch of raised eyebrows. "Nothing worse than a messy pussy." The crude joke got a laugh. He slipped the strap over his neck and started plucking and fine-tuning. The stage lights were still low, making the press of bodies visible if he looked up from his pearl-white Fender P Bass. If he'd pushed, maybe C would have told him her full name and where she lived. Between Toronto and London covered a lot of ground, and he was smack in the middle of it. If she lived close enough, he could have told her where he'd be playing, and...

Get real. Not only was she likely a monster to look at, but she probably lived in some hick-town hours away. And the whole point of chatting on that site was to avoid groupies, not make more. A woman who found him interesting for his brain, who wanted more than to ogle or idolize him, that was what he wanted. Well, that was mostly what he wanted. He'd be strumming another kind of instrument later tonight to take care of the rest.

The house lights dimmed. A rumble erupted from the crowd as the bar manager stepped onstage for the introduction.

"We're packed to capacity tonight, folks. If you don't have a drink yet, flag down one of our beauties and get a couple, because you're gonna need 'em. Our favorite homegrown boys are here to rock you into a hot, sweaty mess. Ladies, and the rest of you ugly lot, give it up for Black Box," he said, then jumped into the mash of patrons.

Applause, screaming, hooting. Travis's adrenaline spiked with the noise. He struck a chord and led the band into their first song, letting the sensations take him over. The neck of the guitar became an extension of his arm. Blood surged through his veins, into the frets, along the strings and back into his body, carrying his soul into the music and the music into his soul. The crowd was there—the electricity of them surrounded him—but he saw nothing. Two songs turned into five, then the bar manager was back, announcing their break.

The stage lights dimmed. Stubbs, their keyboard player, crouched at the edge of the stage. Talking to a woman, of course. Travis slung his guitar aside and sipped ice water, scanning the crowd through lowered eyes. Hundreds of bodies, tons of them women. If he wanted to hook up later, all he had to do was make eye contact with one of them. Or more than one. Been there, done that. Yah, being with more than one woman was hot, no denying that. But all of it had gotten so meaningless. Sex for the sake of getting off, nothing more.

Still, he found himself searching. Tons of women with long, dark hair. Any one of them could be his Scrabble mistress. Or none of them. He'd never know...unless they chatted again and she opened up. Maybe he'd get the ball rolling. Something about her made him want to take the risk.

Behind him, Luke plugged in his guitar and began playing a medley of riffs. Travis joined in, the lights came up and the crowd screeched approval. Not much topped that sound.

They ended the night's performance with the Guns N' Roses cover he'd mentioned to C. He usually went to a totally free place during his solo, but tonight he was thinking of her comment that it was a romantic song. He closed his eyes, tried to conjure an image of his mystery girl. If she was real, the flesh and blood kind of real, he'd play it for her. Acoustic, slowed down to make it sexier. And close up, so they could share the heat of it.

He very much needed to get a grip.

"Dude, come sit at the bar." Victor, Black Box's crazy-ass drummer, poked Travis in the ribs with his drumsticks after their last set had finished. "Bring your strings, chicks love that shit."

"Nah, I'm out of here, for which you should thank me, otherwise I'd steal all the best ones from under that hideous moustache of yours."

Victor laughed, smoothing his fingers over the bushy inverted horseshoe. "The ladies love it. They say it tickles them in all the right places."

"I'll try not to keep that in mind," Travis said as he walked away from Victor, endless free drinks and a sea of liquored-up, willing females.

King Street was wide awake at midnight. The mouth of the club was thick with bodies still waiting to get inside, even though the live music had ended. In his peripheral vision, the building appeared to have puked people onto the concrete. No doubt there'd be plenty of real vomit out there later. Thank god he was past all that.

Back home, he tossed his keys on the table, undressing as he walked through the apartment. He settled on the bed with his laptop, a bottle of water and Kersh—the roomie he'd inherited with the apartment, a black cat that refused to move out no matter how many times he left the door open. At least the place was mouse-free.

"Away from my goods," he said to the kneading feline, tossing the blanket over his lap to be safe. He logged on to the Wordloverz site and off just as quickly. Damn, she wasn't online. He grabbed the pad from the side table, reviewing the notes from their earlier chat. Not much to go on. The strongest clue was the slogan she'd quoted from her workplace. If the business existed, he'd find it. The internet was as much his home as the stage, paying his bills more consistently than his music did. He typed the tagline into the Google search bar. The store had to have a website—everything and everybody had a web presence these days. Hell, he had his share.

"No way." There it was, an independent business with the exact catchphrase. Here, half an hour from his place, max. Less in light traffic. The odds of that had to be miniscule. And she wasn't kidding when she told him they sold the works. Holy shit, it sold some sexy stuff. Critically speaking, the online store looked pretty good. Professional and easy to navigate, though there were places it could have been even better—and would have been, if he'd designed it.

He scrolled through the pages, past lingerie that went from church-lady reserved to porn-star racy, not stopping to look at anything specific until he got to the accessories area. Candles, oils, soaps, jewelry. Nice. Next came the hot stuff—sport sheets for bondage, role-playing get-up. Holy hell, there were a lot of choices. Vibrators, dildos, nipple clamps... and she'd sampled some of this stuff? The images that brought to mind.

It wasn't until Kersh pounced on the blanket that Travis realized more than his mind had wandered. He cursed the cat but couldn't blame him for misinterpreting the kind of playing going on beneath the covers. Yeah, he'd decided. For better or worse, he had to know, had to get a look at the naughty Scrabble vixen. Tomorrow he'd be taking a trip to Romance U.

Sundays tended to be slower at Romance U, despite the impending gift-giving holiday. One of the drawbacks of having an indie shop in the Village, rather than a mall location.

Calli tried to focus on her sister's stories of drinking, dancing and drooling, but her thoughts kept drifting. Part fatigue, part swoony daydreaming. She'd fallen asleep with the laptop open at her side, pathetically hoping Travis would log in for another game. It was all she could do not to go to the Wordloverz site right now. Only Caitlyn's intermittent presence in the doorway to the back office kept Calli semi-focused on work.

Her distracted state seemed to go unnoticed. Rare, given Caitlyn seldom missed a trick. Her sister's ability to read people is what made her a killer salesperson, not to mention wildly popular with pretty much anyone who ever met her, male or female. She was the perfect chameleon—comfortably becoming exactly what the person standing next to her wanted her to be. Not that Calli was jealous. Much.

At ten-to-closing time, the overhead bell chimed. Calli expected Caitlyn to mutter curses under her breath, but whoever had walked through the front door elicited an excited gasp instead. Had to be an attractive male customer. The problem with those, though—according to Caitlyn—was that they were in the store to shop for some other woman. Temporarily, at least. Caitlyn usually got what she wanted in the end. Especially when the *what* was a *who* equipped with eyes and a penis.

"My day just got a whole lot more exciting," Caitlyn said, then disappeared into the store.

Caitlyn's laughter was giddy, less controlled than usual. This guy must be something, having that kind of effect on a seasoned pro.

Calli rolled her chair across the room and peeked out. Officially, they were discussing candles, but Caitlyn's body language clearly indicated she was selling something else. And no wonder, the man was gorgeous. Thirty-ish, with short hair the color of hot fudge. A little bit of scruff on his jaw and neck—sexy stubble, not the kind a man would have because he was simply too lazy to shave. He'd probably shaved this morning, but had so much testosterone that it'd already started to fill in. Even from her hiding spot, Calli could see the confidence oozing from him. And sex appeal. Lots of it.

That familiar pang of green gnawed at her gut. She'd never experience what hid so tantalizingly beneath those low-slung jeans. Even if she ran out there naked, his warm, sparkling eyes would still focus on Caitlyn. How could they not?

Being the plain sister, the invisible one, had always meant going unnoticed a lot. Like now, which was a good thing, in its own whacked way. She slipped into the main store, inching closer, then kneeling to fold product that gave her access without drawing attention. The voyeur in her couldn't resist the show.

"So it's Caitlyn—with a C," the delectable guy said as he looked up from the engraved nametag adorning Caitlyn's massive boobage.

"Since the day I was born." Caitlyn didn't waver a millimeter under his gaze.

"Finding you was easier than I thought. Thanks for leaving me a good clue."

"I'm glad you got it, I wasn't sure."

The guy unleashed a smile that would melt the panties off a lifelong, menopausal nun. Thank god she was already on the ground because Calli's knees dissolved at the sight. She could only imagine the effect at close range, yet Caitlyn looked self-assured as ever. Oh, to have an ounce of her confidence.

"I take notes when I'm interested." His smile went from sexy to shy, which, on him, was equally as sexy. The man was sexy, sexy, sexy. That was all. "And last night, you definitely caught my interest."

"Let me grab my purse and jacket, we can grab a coffee... or something." Caitlyn didn't wait for his answer before turning away. She was in the back office looking around when Calli snuck back through the doorway. "What the heck were you doing, spying?"

"Guilty. Sorry."

Caitlyn's smile was huge. "Don't worry, I'd spy on you too, if the situation were reversed. God, he's even hotter than he was last night."

As if their situation would ever be reversed. Calli stuck close to the opening so she could continue to look at the current example of Caitlyn's good fortune. "You met him at the bar, I assume. Geez, you weren't kidding about the guys that go there."

"The place was packed, tons of good pickings, but he," Caitlyn pointed toward the front room, "was far and away the best. Some guitarists are so into their damn instruments, they might as well be alone in a room as onstage before an audience. This one was the opposite. He really connected with the audience, and I swear he kept looking at me. So I left a note with the bartender. You never know when you're going to get lucky, right? But then he took off immediately after their last set. I figured either he didn't get it or he wasn't actually staring at me. Sooo glad I was wrong."

Something curled in Calli's stomach, and it wasn't the egg-salad sandwich she'd had for lunch. Food poisoning or a viral infection would be a short-term problem. Either was preferable to the gut-twisting reality check now in progress.

While she'd been randomly chatting with some anonymous and possibly grotesque guitar player—if he even *was* a guitar player—her sister had been catching the eye of a very tangible, very sexy one. Caitlyn's follow-up date was sure to singe the sheets. The only thing Calli would be burning up later was batteries. At least she had rechargeables.

"You really should've come with, Cal. You would've loved the music...and the guys." Caitlyn adjusted the short leather jacket that matched her spike-heeled over-the-knee boots. She applied more blood-red lipstick and winked at Calli. "Talk to you tomorrow, hopefully with oodles of juicy details."

Calli followed her sister through the archway. Caitlyn

and the customer-who-wasn't-really-a-customer had their backs to her. Calli saw a wedge of his killer smile as he held the door open. He bent his head to Caitlyn and said something that Calli couldn't make out. Caitlyn laughed and called him a weirdo, squeezing his biceps. The door closed after them, leaving Calli alone, surrounded by products she'd never share with anybody but customers.

Just this once, Calli hoped Caitlyn would keep the juicy details to herself.

Another time, Travis would've been counting his good luck, sitting across from Caitlyn. Not tonight.

She wasn't what he'd expected. The woman in front of him matched the basic description—long brown hair and blue eyes. She had a first name starting with C and her last name was Yates, another match to the hints from last night. The location was right. She was pretty, as he'd hoped she would be. Sexy too. But something was off.

For one, she hadn't been at all surprised to see him standing in the lingerie—correction, romance—store. Sure, she'd left a trail of crumbs in their chat, but he'd gotten the impression she didn't expect him to follow. The woman sitting across the table acted as though she'd been waiting for him.

Number two, she wasn't getting any of the references he'd made to their online conversation. Instead, she kept changing the subject to last night's performance at The Cove. Compliments on his guitar playing, accompanied by allusions to fucking him. His dick wasn't missing those suggestions. He shifted in his chair and racked his brain for an unsexy thought. Had one, pussy of another kind. Kersh's litter box was overdue for scooping. He smiled and took another stab at directing their conversation out of the bar. And the bedroom.

"How long have you worked at the romance store?"

"Since it opened two years ago." Caitlyn pushed her latte aside and crossed her arms on the table, providing a direct view into her ample cleavage. "Next time you come by I'll give you the VIP tour."

Travis forced his eyes upward. "Daytime, or after hours?"

"Daytime, unfortunately. The owner lives upstairs and she's always there, especially at night."

"Not a big fan of your boss, I gather."

"Actually I'm her biggest fan." Caitlyn sat back in her chair. "I work for my sister. She's wicked-smart about business, a talented designer and probably the sweetest person I've ever known."

Finally, real communication. "But?"

"But she needs to get out of that building and live a little." She leaned forward again, raking her eyes over him and licking her lips. Her hand slid over his. "The store is full of goodies that should be used for pleasure, not just profit."

And…she was back on the prowl. He should be hustling Caitlyn and her shiny red lips out to his Nissan. Lord knows his lower body wanted him to, but it was no longer in charge of his actions. Unfortunately for his dick, his head still wasn't convinced. For the sake of his balls he dangled another fragment of their online banter. Whether the boys went without tonight depended on Caitlyn's reaction as much as her answer.

"All in the name of market research?" he asked, quoting C Ya's line from their online chat. Caitlyn blinked, then blinked again, oblivious. Travis guessed she was no stranger to a good time. Maybe she'd been drunk or high last night and had no recollection of their chat. He stood and shoved his hands into his front pockets, then nodded toward the café windows. "The weather isn't getting any better. I can give you a lift to your car if you need one."

"I'm good, thanks." She gave him a smile that said, *last chance or you'll miss out, buddy.*

Travis bet she was right. Big time. He watched her shrug on a jacket that had no intention of providing warmth against the biting November wind. When he offered a handshake, her eyes opened wide and her lower lip dropped a fraction of an inch. He pasted on his practiced fan-face, a look that was friendly and calm without offering any false hope. Inside, he was as confused as she looked.

"Thanks for the coffee, it was nice to meet you," she said, sounding as though they'd just finished an interview.

Travis gave her hand a gentle squeeze. "You too. Sorry it didn't work out the way we expected." Or the way he'd hoped.

She leaned in to kiss his cheek. "If *your* expectations change, you know how to find me."

You know how to find me. Same words as last night, but coming from a completely different woman, or so it seemed. He watched her through the plate glass, jacket open despite the blatant threat of sleeting rain. Chin up and chest out, Caitlyn didn't walk, she strutted. As she should, the woman was definitely sexy. The woman who'd captured his attention online was also sexy, in a more subtle way. Travis doubted Caitlyn had a subtle cell in her voluptuous body.

Collar turned up to his ears, Travis darted to his car, cursing the drop in temperature since entering the coffee house. He pulled on the toque stashed in the glove box and blew on his hands while waiting for the heat.

One of three things had happened. The first option—in the limited course of their online chat he'd misinterpreted her personality. Second, her demure side had given way to predatory instinct when she learned he was in a band. A conceited thought, but it'd happened more than once.

Or third, Caitlyn and C Ya weren't the same woman. That one took coincidental to an insane level. Still, it was his favorite theory because it kept the ball in play.

His own balls continued to protest the lonely night ahead. They hadn't had the pleasure of female contact in a couple of months. An eternity ago.

"Sorry, boys," he mused as he pulled away from the curb. "But we're waiting for the right woman, for once." Tonight's agenda included testing his hypothesis. And a cold shower, though not necessarily in that order.

Chapter Three

Calli rubbed her temples. She had to stay up a bit longer. Until the little men with sledgehammers stopped trying to crack her skull open from the inside. Her fault for having more than one glass of wine at her pity party. Another thing she didn't do as well as her sister—handle alcohol.

She propped up against a bank of pillows and opened the laptop. Her personal inbox was always a lifeless place, save messages from spammers trying to sell her Viagra and discounted evening gowns. Having use for either of those things would be great. Both in one evening—even better. A girl could dream, if nothing else.

The business inbox was also quiet. No orders, no inquiries. Not legit ones. Just a single message detailing what the sender wanted to do with particular items from the online store. The third email of its type in a week. Each came from a different address, but the tone and voice were the same, and the content was getting more perverted. More personal. A shiver ran up Calli's spine. Thank god her name wasn't listed anywhere on the website.

Too bad the only dirty emails she received came from some disgusting stranger. She wouldn't mind if Travis sent her sexually suggestive emails...

Travis. In reality, he probably wasn't half as good-looking as Caitlyn's date. The more Calli thought about that, the more she liked the idea. She still hoped the guitar-playing part was true, but on a smaller scale than Caitlyn's hunky musician. Some out-of-the-way, reserved venue, not onstage at one of Caitlyn's monstrous hangouts. Her sister could have all the jaw-dropping, larger-than-life front men. Calli'd never be able to handle a man like that.

She scanned the open games on the Wordloverz site. No avatars jumped out at her as Travis's black rose had. Moping over a guy she didn't know and had played one game with was ridiculous.

"Let's try this and see what happens..." She clicked a few boxes and started a public game. Then she did what came naturally—she waited.

By the time she'd retrieved soda crackers from the kitchen, an animated host had popped onto the screen, holding a message card.

Travis has accepted your invitation. Accept this player or decline?

The black rose sat below her red rose. Travis. Somewhere out there he was seeing a similar screen... and waiting for her to click the play button.

Butterflies swirled in her stomach as she surveyed her tiles. The cursor blinked in the chat window, inviting her to play another kind of game. Her fingers hovered over the keyboard. What to say? A simple hello, something more flirtatious?

Charming jumped down from the bed and began tap dancing on the worn hardwood floor. Calli shot him a look. Great timing, little dog.

"Go to your pan." The command fell on stubborn, pointy ears. Charming hated doing his business indoors. She'd chosen a Chihuahua largely for the breed's willingness to be litter-box trained. Charming never messed on her floors or furniture, but only used the litter pan as a last resort. He'd acquiesced to the training, not to preferring the method. Meaning she had to haul her ass off the bed and take him out. Or try to.

The closer she got to the door, the more her stomach knotted. She flipped on the exterior lights. Slid the chain across and let it dangle. She put her hand on the deadbolt, paused and took several deep breaths. She could do this. Nothing to be scared of. The lock clicked open in her shaking hand. She could do this.

Slowly, she opened the door that led to the rear of the building. Not dark at all, thanks to those extra spotlights she'd had installed. But when she looked up, the sky was nothing but black. No stars in sight, the moon hidden by dark clouds. That same blackness lay beyond the illuminated patch of property, wrapping around everything and everyone who stepped out into the night. A mugger could be anywhere—close enough to reach her before she could make it back to the door. Oh god... she couldn't do this.

She crouched inside the doorframe. "Charming, hurry up..." she urged as her little dog used his sixteen-foot flexible leash to wander around, sniffing leisurely. "Come on, boy, do your job... please."

Voices filtered through the night air from the street out front. Her stomach lurched into her throat. Faster than she could tell him to come, she reeled the Chihuahua back into the building. Slammed the door, locked the locks and sank to her knees.

One year, eleven months, twenty-four days. She hadn't set foot outside after dark for almost two years. The fear was as paralyzing now as it had been the day she came home from the hospital. Maybe it would be for the rest of her life. How could she get past it when her attacker was still out there, wandering the streets, looking like any average, non-threatening guy? The alley he'd dragged her into was a ten-minute walk from here... That man—that monster—could live in the neighborhood for all she knew.

"Sorry, buddy," she said as her dog skulked toward his indoor toilet. And she was. More than the little canine would ever know.

In her now-sucky mood, she flopped on the bed with her laptop and played the word *alone*. Totally appropriate.

He must have been waiting, because the chat window went active immediately. ***Took you long enough to come up with that.***

The cursor blinked impatiently. She'd been itching for this opportunity since last night, and now she had nothing witty or interesting to say. She sighed and banged a boring message into the box. ***My dog needed to visit his favorite lamppost before getting into bed with me.***

Does he sleep under the covers or on top?

Under, between my knees.

Is he cuddled up next to flannel or silk?

A couple of messages from Travis and her mood had already turned around. Calli smiled and hit send on her fib. ***Neither... skin.***

Damn. That's one lucky dog.

The happy butterflies in her stomach went into full flutter. *For all you know, my legs are like a gorilla's and my hygiene habits are lacking.*

For all you know, I'm into malodorous, hairy women.

Once again, her mystery man had her laughing out loud. Her laptop chimed as a word appeared on the game board. *Stinky.*

She giggled at the screen. *I can't believe you played the K for single points. A cute move, but I guess you're not playing to win tonight.*

I always win, sweetheart.

Holy arrogant.

I prefer to look at it as goal-minded and success-oriented.

Ooh, that was almost as hot as the guitar playing and hints of dominance. God, she was such a geek. *That's a serious approach for a silly Scrabble game.*

There's nothing silly about this game. I've been looking forward to it since eight thirty last night.

Another flip-floppy thing happened in Calli's stomach. *Haven't you played with anyone else since then?*

No. I was waiting for you.

Should I be flattered, creeped-out or call bullshit?

It's the truth. Guess that leaves you with two options, C.

In that case, I'll go with... She hit send on the message, then on her move—*blushed.*

Travis played *cute.* She found a spot on the board

and followed with *you*. Neither of them was going to set a point record this game. She raised an eyebrow at his next word—*come*.

That's one of my favorite words. She hit send before chickening out.

Mine too. Want to?

Was he suggesting cyber-sex? Virtual or otherwise, she didn't have a clue how to begin. She'd never had an orgasm with a man, not even close. Her limited sexual encounters had all been so awkward and fast, she hadn't even had time to fake an orgasm.

But she had to say something... *Yes.*

Good. Come over and play with me. I'll let you go first.

She had the perfect comeback for that one. *Just once, or every time?*

Each and every time, sweetheart.

Calli fanned herself. Okay, they definitely weren't talking about Scrabble. Since it wasn't real, she dove right in. *Can I bring my dog?*

Only if he won't eat my cat. On second thought, only if he will eat my cat.

You're horrible! My dog is only eight pounds. He'd probably be terrified of your cat. Another fib. Charming would take any excuse to get out of the apartment, cat or no cat.

They'd make a great pair. My cat fears nothing. He could be the bodyguard.

I could use a bodyguard. Maybe I'll hire your cat.

Travis played another move, then his message popped up. *Lazy cat'd probably fall asleep on the job. I, on the other hand, would stay up all night guarding your body.*

Well now, this was getting interesting. *Now I feel very, um, safe.*

So I have the job? Should I bring any special gear— pepper spray, a gun, handcuffs...

You happen to have those things lying around?

Not the pepper spray or a gun. I could improvise and bring my guitar.

But he owned handcuffs? Oh boy. The Kalahari was wet in comparison to Calli's mouth. Conditions south of the border were anything but desert-like.

So if somebody breaks in downstairs, your plan is to serenade him, then cuff him?

Sure, but that would be a waste of both the serenading and the handcuffs.

Wasn't that the truth? Far-off as it surely was, Calli pictured the hottie who'd visited her sister earlier. Imagined him as her Scrabble-playing Travis, sitting on her bed, playing guitar just for her. Then, after the song was over, he'd set the instrument aside. Pull the handcuffs from his back pocket. He'd stretch her hands up over her head, and... Whoa. Not the time to get lost in a hot bondage fantasy.

Speaking of serenading, how was work last night? There, a safe, respectable message.

Audience was great. I split after the last song, hoping to catch you online when I got home, but no such luck. You were probably out.

If you mean out cold, you're right, I stayed in and fell asleep on the couch. I checked for you after I finished work tonight, but you weren't online. God, she sounded like a desperate hermit. Which she was, but he didn't need to know that side of her. Only the person she wished she could be.

I was having coffee around five, but it didn't work out the way I expected.

Odd comment. How did a coffee not work out— what did he expect it to do for him, anyway?

Calli shrugged and sent a boring, truthful answer. *I never touch the stuff. I'm strictly an herbal tea girl.*

Travis cracked his knuckles. Progress, excellent. His crazy theory that Caitlyn and C Ya were two separate women was true.

Both he and Caitlyn were at The Cove last night, but C was asleep on her couch, probably with a dog between her legs. And while he and Caitlyn were having the world's most awkward cup of joe late this afternoon, C was online, looking for him. Plus, she didn't drink coffee, whereas Caitlyn had downed most of an extra-large latte in their short time together. On top of that, Caitlyn had told him that she worked for her sister, which meant another female with the last name Yates worked at the romance store. All good signs.

If he didn't break through in the music business, maybe he should take up detective work as a sideline to his freelance website jobs. Yeah, probably not.

Now he had to decide on a move, and not only for the game board. Something to make her spill some information. *Where do you go for tea?*

To my office.

Not giving him an inch, was she? He couldn't come out and tell her he'd figured out where she worked. Not unless he wanted her to bolt. Hell, he'd flip the fuck out if he found out some chick was creeping the web, essentially stalking him.

You have one of those bosses who won't let you out of the building?

Something like that.

He played the word *date* and sent a message, hoping she'd put the two together. *How about after work sometime?*

The moves kept coming, but no reply. No chat at all. As the board filled and the available tiles diminished, Travis's stomach tightened. He had a few plays left. A couple of minutes at best before the game ended. She might've ignored his question, or it could've been a glitch. He'd only know if he sent another message.

His fingers hovered over the keys. And he had... nothing. Nothing good, anyway. Damn it. *Are you working tomorrow?*

Yes, by myself. Monday is one of the slow days. Boring and long.

Perfect. Thank you, C, for that little tidbit. *Maybe tomorrow will be different. You never know, something exciting could happen.*

Freelancing had its drawbacks, namely the occasional dry spells between projects, but it came with a lot of perks. Like being able to walk into Romance U in the middle of a Monday afternoon.

Travis's pulse picked up a few beats, more than it had when he approached the same threshold twenty-four hours ago. Yesterday's trip had been to check a hunch. Today was a sure thing.

He paused outside. The sun had come out after lunch, reflecting so brilliantly off the layer of fresh snow, he'd needed sunglasses. He pushed them to the top of his head. He wanted a clear view when he walked through the door.

An electronic chime announced his arrival. A woman sat behind the main counter, bowed over a book, dark hair pooling on newsprint as her pencil tapped frenetically on the gleaming white countertop. He'd made it halfway into the store before she raised her head, looked him in the eye and straightened on her stool. The sight stopped him mid-step.

He'd hoped she'd be attractive. Expected it, since her sister was a looker. But he hadn't prepared himself for the possibility that his anonymous Scrabble crush would be knockout beautiful.

She'd given him limited details about her appearance, not enough to form a good mental picture. Very long dark hair, fair skin and blue eyes—all true. And too simplistic to do her justice. Sleek, shiny hair the color of black coffee hung straight. Down her back on one side, completely covering her chest on the other.

He loved long hair on women, and hers was incredible. She wore bangs, a thick fringe in a crisp line at eyebrow level. All that dark hair in contrast to her smooth, creamy complexion...he couldn't take his eyes off her, she was so stunning.

But there was something else. More than the pretty picture staring him down as he approached. She had this...damn, there was *something* about her. Eyes full of fire, sexy curves all buttoned and tucked neatly away inside a sweet, innocent exterior. Just looking at her messed with his wiring. He wasn't sure what he wanted to do more—adore her or corrupt her.

"Can I help you?"

Hell yes, she could help him. Give him a sec and he'd hand her a list of the ways.

With her delicate features and soft eyes, he'd expected a high, singsong voice, not the throaty lower register that'd slipped through her pale-pink lips. Damn sexy. Decision made. He'd adore her, absolutely, but he'd do it while corrupting her—every way possible.

"You can," he said, glancing at the engraved badge secured to her blouse. No name. Just, *Manager*. Not so helpful. "I'm looking for someone."

"Sure." Her eyes flitted around the store as she spoke, never landing on him for more than a second at a time. "For a new girlfriend, wife...same-sex partner?"

The laugh came out so hard, it choked him. "I don't have any of those to shop for. I meant literally—I'm here to see Ms. Yates."

"Sorry, Caitlyn doesn't work until Thursday." She pushed a notepad with the store's insignia in his direction. "If you'd like to leave a message, I'll make sure she gets it as soon as possible."

Was that frost in her voice? Possibly, if her sister had recounted the awkward coffee shop non-date. Coming in here yesterday—all cocky and inadequately informed—was effectively biting him in the ass. Now he had to overcome the obstacle of sort of hitting on her sister—a moment the real C Ya had obviously witnessed, unbeknownst to him. Damn fine mess he'd made.

"Not Caitlyn. Nice girl, but that was a miscommunication. I'm here to see her sister—you."

Now her gaze stayed on his face. Up close, the blue was almost gray, with lashes that'd make any woman envious.

She flipped her hair over her shoulder. Drilled him with a wary look and crossed her arms, an act that squeezed her chest higher and tighter against the white blouse. She might be trying to hide behind all those buttons, but the thin fabric had other ideas. Such as showing off her bra. Light-pink with tiny polka dots and a lacy edge.

God help him, he was already picturing her in her underwear, those nice, full tits straining to escape silky cups—and he had a hard-on to show for it. If he had to leave the shelter of the counter in the next few minutes, he was in trouble.

"Why do you want to see *me*?"

His solid plan to get to know her before revealing their online connection had died the second he realized she'd seen him with Caitlyn yesterday. Now it was full-disclosure time.

"To bring you these." He set a takeout cup on the counter, then pulled a vintage portable Scrabble game from his inner coat pocket and placed it beside the herbal tea. "And to make your long, boring Monday a bit more exciting."

Chapter Four

"Oh my god..." Calli stepped backward until the floor-to-ceiling shelving thumped her in the hip, ending her retreat. "You're...him." No way, not possible. She pinched her eyes closed, shook her head, then looked again. Yep, he was still there, totally gorgeous, looking at her with the most amazing hazel eyes she'd ever seen. "*You're* him?"

"Travis Graham," he extended his right hand, "unless you'd rather call me Scrabble Master T."

She stared at the hand he'd offered. Stared and stared, but it didn't drop away. Her palms slid against the shelf she was clutching. Shaking anybody's hand, especially his, was out of the question.

How had he found her, and a better question, why? Thanks to a conversation with Caitlyn, Calli knew his claim to be a guitarist was true—his band played to packed clubs. Caitlyn had been ready to jump into his bed yesterday and he'd turned her down. Because he'd realized that Caitlyn wasn't...*her*? This had to be some kind of joke.

She twisted to peer out the window. No suspicious vans that could be housing hidden camera crews. No signs of life at all. Just the tall, handsome one standing in front of her, waiting for her to shake his hand. She let go of the wall unit and wiped the sweat on her skirt as subtly as possible. She inched forward, forcing her hand to extend when she got within contact distance.

Nope. Still couldn't do it. "So it's true that you play guitar," she said, snatching the drink instead. She peeled back the sipping tab, then pressed it closed again. They'd chatted online. Her sister had no qualms about him, obviously. And while she couldn't recall exactly what her attacker in the alley had looked like, she was damn sure Travis wasn't that guy. Didn't mean she was ready to drink some mystery beverage he plunked on her counter, though.

He let his hands drop to the counter, little crinkles forming at the corners of his eyes as he watched her playing with the cup. "Yes. Mostly bass with the band. When I'm writing music, or playing strictly for personal enjoyment, I prefer acoustic."

Not just a guitarist, a songwriter. Yes, apparently Travis Graham *could* get even hotter. "And you really do have a beaten-up Scrabble board."

"I do." His fingers tapped a beat on the faded burgundy vinyl cover of the collapsible board.

If hands could be sexy, Travis's were. So was his smile. Warm and genuine, it started with his lips and went all the way to his eyes. Totally disarming…and knee-melting. She couldn't help but relax. Just a little.

"Where's your third arm?"

"Inside my coat. I had a special pocket added for it." He nodded in her direction. "You must have a good dentist—those teeth look almost real."

Ooh, he was quick. But she could be too. She pointed to where his coat hung open. "I bet that tight t-shirt really chafes your giant mole."

"Nice legs," he said while leaning in and totally checking her out. "Not gorilla-like at all."

She giggled, then slapped a hand over her mouth to squelch the foreign sound. When was the last time a man had made her giggle? God, she couldn't remember, not a single time.

"You have a nice laugh." His fingers gently wrapped around her wrist and pulled her hand away. "A pretty smile too."

Her brain quit the second he touched her. Apparently it couldn't function at the same time as her libido, which was running wild with possibilities that'd never come true.

"You still haven't told me your first name."

With his thumb making circles over her pulse point, she barely *remembered* her name. The adrenaline rushing through her veins wasn't entirely excitement. Travis was handsome, sexy, funny and charming. But he was also a virtual stranger who'd sought her out without permission or notice.

Okay, that wasn't entirely true—he *had* invited her to go on a date during their last game. It'd been vague and she'd assumed he was kidding—because how could it have been real? Now she knew. He'd already figured out where she worked. Then there'd been the comment about how today might not be so boring. He'd given her some clues of his own, hadn't he? If he meant to hurt her, he'd have snuck up on her, not walked through the front door—twice.

"How did you find me?"

"Simple Google search. You told me an approximate location and quoted me the tagline of the place you work, which turned out to be unique to this store."

"Oh god... what was I thinking?" She'd been so stupid and careless. Anybody could've found her with the info she'd given up. Travis wasn't a psycho—probably—but if she'd chatted with somebody else, somebody less... upfront... She covered her throat with her free hand. Tried deep breathing to beat back the panic, but couldn't get enough air into her lungs.

"Whoa, you okay?" He caught her mid-swoon, the act bringing them into a clinch. Subtly applied cologne infiltrated her nose, adding to her dizziness. Heat tickled her thighs, her belly, the untouched country in between.

"Not really," she whispered, utterly lost in his eyes. Understatement of the year on more levels than she could count at the moment.

"I probably moved too fast. I do that when I want something."

"And you wanted *me*? Sight unseen, based on a couple of chats during a Scrabble game? I don't get it, I mean, look at you..." Her eyes flitted over every inch she could see, given their close proximity. "And you're a musician, practically a rock star."

His jaw ticked. Arms stiffened where they held her. For a second Calli thought he might drop her on her ass and walk out the door. And she didn't like the idea.

"Are you..." How to word it. How to ask if the ridiculously good-looking man holding her in his arms was some nut-job stalker. "Insane?"

"Not currently. I've been on the wagon for almost two months." Dear god, he had dimples to go with the charming crinkles when he smiled.

She was such a goner.

"Very reassuring." She couldn't help it, she trusted that smile. Probably because she *was* insane. She took a step back before completely losing her mind and melting into him. Didn't let go of his hand, though. That amount of crazy she'd keep. "Seriously. Why'd you come looking for me?"

"Didn't have a choice after those chats, sweetheart. I had to know if the funny, sexy girl I met online was real."

Words to give her a wake-up call. She *was* that girl from the chats—on the inside. Day-to-day, though, not even close. He'd realize that the minute he asked her to leave this building with him. No point in letting this fantasy go one step further.

She removed her hand from Travis's grip and pushed the Scrabble board toward him. "Sorry to disappoint you, but she's not."

Leftover stir-fry wasn't hitting the spot tonight. Nothing was.

Calli scraped the food into the trash can, rinsed her dishes and flopped on the couch. The laptop taunted her from the coffee table. So did the Scrabble board Travis had refused to take when she asked him to leave the store. Because he only wanted to play with her, he'd said, before walking out the door.

Travis had looks. He had talent and intelligence. This was a man who could have his pick of women and probably did, on a regular basis. Why he was intent on *her* made no sense at all.

Maybe he had a weird fetish for nerdy, plain girls. Even so, she still couldn't have him. Unless he had a very specific fetish for nerdy, plain girls who don't go out after dark. Ugh.

Even if she wasn't a neurotic mess, he was still miles out of her league. How could she relax and be... fun... if he was in front of her, looking right at her? Yet somehow she'd managed today. She'd flirted. She'd joked. She'd even laughed. Travis, barely more than a stranger, flipped that switch for her. Freed her to be more than boringly basic.

And god, she wanted more of that feeling.

Charming grumbled as she moved him aside to reach for the laptop. She drilled her fingernails against the plastic housing while the computer started up. Slow much? She'd bought it with her business startup loan two years ago. Too soon to justify an upgrade. Funny, she'd never noticed the lag time before. Just thinking about chatting with Travis had her fidgety. Her fingers stumbled, hitting the wrong keys, hitting Enter before she'd input her password.

"Stupid fingers." Her heart zoomed. Premature anticipation—he might not be online. Worse, he might not want to play with her after her spaz moment this afternoon.

Finally, the page loaded. The black rose popped onto the screen, a red bubble beside it indicating he'd invited her to a game. Three hours ago, if the timestamp was correct. *After* she'd booted him from Romance U. No message waiting for her in the chat pane, not that she expected one. That move was on her.

She played the best word she could with her crummy one-point tiles, then typed a message. **My name is Calli.**

His reply popped up immediately, as if he'd been waiting for her. Unbelievable. **A beautiful name for a beautiful girl.**

For some reason, she believed he meant it. "Ooh, charming, aren't you?" She'd spoken to the screen, but her four-legged friend didn't understand as much. He'd heard his name and now he wanted attention—of the *take me outside* variety. She fixed him with a glare, useless at it was. Charming's head fit in the palm of her hand but his stubborn streak was a mile wide. "Your timing stinks worse than your poop."

She typed, **I have to take my dog out…don't go anywhere, okay?**

Nowhere else I want to be, Calli.

Seeing him use her name gave her a boost. Too bad she'd been her typical cowardly self this afternoon. If she'd told him her name then, she would've gotten to hear him say it in his deep, smooth voice. Maybe she still would. A girl could dream.

The day had been sunny, but the evening was bone-chillingly windy. Snow whipped inside when she opened the door for Charming. Even he wanted no part of stepping out into that weather, opting to voluntarily use his indoor facilities instead. Thank you, small miracles.

Not only had Travis waited, he'd left her a message.

Are you still wearing that white blouse and checkered skirt?

Checkered. She shook her head. *It's houndstooth, not checkered. But yes.*

I stand corrected. You looked incredible. You have perfect legs for a short skirt like that. And all those little pearls buttoned up to your chin... very sexy.

Sexy? Her? In this outfit? Not hardly. *Do you always drink during the daytime, or just today?*

I don't drink. I like being in full control.

Oh, well. She was definitely in favor of Travis being in full control.

He played the word *ravish*, then another message appeared on his side of the chat window. *That's what I wanted to do when you crossed your arms at me. Pop every last one of those damn buttons. Put my hands and lips all over what you're hiding under there.*

Her nipples tightened and a wave of heat spread from her belly to her thighs. No man had ever expressed a desire like that to her. About her.

What about my skirt? Would you have left that on? She gasped at the sight of her words on the screen. God, she was really doing this—dirty chatting with Travis, who was no longer a faceless, anonymous man but a six-foot slab of yumminess who'd actually touched her a few hours ago.

After I slipped the shirt down your arms, I'd touch, kiss and lick every inch of your creamy skin until you begged me to take off that polka-dot bra I caught a glimpse of. I'd trace your curves, the outline of your nipples. First with my finger, then my tongue, until your nipples were hard and aching for me to suck them. And while I was kissing and nibbling your nipples, I'd ease the zipper down on your houndstooth (not checkered) skirt. I'd slide it over your hips and let it hit the floor. I'd run my hands over your ass, down the back of your legs, up the inside of your thighs.

"And then what?" The cursor blinked, but nothing else popped up in answer. Ten seconds, thirty, a full minute. Still nothing. *Are you still there?*

Yeah.

I thought maybe you got disconnected.

No, Calli, I'm waiting for you.

To do what? This is where being one of the world's most inexperienced thirty-one-year-olds became glaringly obvious. She didn't have a clue what she was supposed to have done.

To tell me to keep going. That you want more.

I thought you liked having full control.

I do. But I'll only ever do things you want.

Oh god. It was as if he knew her secret desires. *I want. Don't stop.*

Take off your blouse and skirt. Keep the bra and panties.

She didn't ask why. Just did as he'd asked, or rather, told. Goose bumps rippled over her arms, breasts and stomach as she got next-to-naked in her living room for a man who couldn't see her.

I took them off. And left them on.

Good. I wish I could see you.

Me too. Knowing it wasn't going to happen made it easy to say.

Where are you—at a desk, in bed?

On my couch with the laptop.

Put it beside you. Lick your fingertips and touch your nipples. Play with them. Squeeze them. Until they're so hard it's almost unbearable to touch them anymore.

She slipped her fingers inside her bra. Her nipples were already hard, they'd been that way since he first mentioned control. Still, she obeyed, rubbing and tickling her breasts. Plucking her nipples until the lightest touch made her jerk.

They're so hard…I don't think they've ever been this hard before.

Does it feel good?

God yes. It feels so good. I never touch them this much. She pictured him smiling at that, then tugged at them again.

Do you wish it was me touching them?

Mind reader. **Yes.**

If I were with you, I wouldn't stop at your breasts. I'd be sliding my hand down your stomach right now…under the edge of your panties. Describe them to me.

Calli tipped her head for a better look. Not the most risqué pair she owned, but cute. **They're low-rise boy-cut shorts with a little bow on the front. They match the bra.**

Very nice. Sexy in an innocent way, like you.

She slipped one hand under the polka-dotted fabric and headed straight for her clit. Touching herself in the middle of the living room. With the lights on, while sexting with a hot bass player who for some unfathomable reason was interested in her. Interested enough to seek her out and come bearing a Scrabble board. Crazy. Crazier yet was hitting send on the message she'd pecked with her free hand.

It's wet in my panties. Hot too.

You're killing me.

Want me to stop?

Not a fucking chance, sweetheart. I want you to finger yourself until you come. I want you to tell me exactly what you're doing and how it feels.

Only if you do the same.

You want me to finger myself?

She pictured him grinning at the screen... the sexy smile lines by his almond-shaped eyes, the slight dimples in his cheeks. *If that's how you like it...*

I think I'll go with stroking instead.

She hadn't asked where he lived, but it couldn't be too far, since he'd dropped by the store twice in as many days. Right now he might as well be in the room. Heat washed over her at the mental image of Travis, legs extended, cock in his hand. His eyes would be on her while he palmed his length, over and over.

She circled her clit, brushing her fingertips over it at the top of each pass. Lightly at first, harder as the need to come surged. She ditched the teasing circles for full-contact rubbing, edging closer and closer to climax with each second.

Until the laptop beeped at her. **Calli. Talk to me.**

She groaned and pecked out a quick message. **Can't type while I'm...you know. Need another hand.**

Travis's reply was immediate. **I have two you can use.**

So come over and use them, why don't you? She sent the message before she could overthink it. Putting the invitation out there was safe enough—he knew where she worked, not where she lived.

If he did accept, she could play it off as part of their sexy little game. She didn't have to take it further. Though if he asked for her address, she might just give it up, have Travis over...for sex. Even if for one time. So what if she'd never done anything like this before.

I'll be there in twenty minutes. And Calli...put your clothes back on. I want to enjoy undoing those buttons for myself.

He'd what? Be here in twenty minutes, to undress her? Impossible.

Think, think...in any of their chats, had she given clues about living above the store? Her skin tingled from the self-inflicted pleasure-teasing and now, from frazzled nerves. She jumped off the couch. Paced while racking her brain. No, she definitely hadn't told him. Her home phone had a private listing that didn't come up in searches. He couldn't know.

She plunked onto the couch and hauled the computer onto her lap. Oh god. He'd logged out. That could only mean one thing—he was on his way. Here, to her place.

Somehow, he knew. Meaning she had about eighteen minutes to decide whether to answer her door.

Travis bumped the wipers from intermittent to steady speed. The snow was really coming down now and it was the wet kind. *Wet.* When Calli had sent that message about her wet panties, then disappeared from their chat to play with herself… he'd gone from a basic hard-on to a steel beam. Given her one-eighty this afternoon, there was a damn good chance she'd have changed her mind about her invitation by the time he got to her place. If so, his shower had an unlimited supply of cold, *wet* water.

From his conversation with Caitlyn, he knew Calli lived above Romance U. Few of the indie stores along Belmont had parking lots, so he found a spot on the street. The store was dark. The upper windows were dark. But what did he expect—that she'd be standing on the sidewalk waiting for him?

Yeah, maybe he did expect that, since he'd gotten used to women falling all over him. At gigs, in emails, the daily comments on the band's blog and Facebook page— offers no red-blooded male should refuse.

Like his band-mates, he'd enjoyed his fair share of those offers. Enjoyed every carnal act he'd ever wanted, then walked without a single look back. How many women had he fucked and left? Hell if he even knew. But Calli wasn't one of those women. He was a cocky idiot for expecting her to act like one.

He cursed the sleet that slapped him in the face as he scoured the building for a second entrance. Should've asked. He'd been so damn eager to grab her invitation and run with it. Now he had to skulk around in the dark. Served him right.

Long, narrow alleys divided the old buildings in this section of the city. Barely wide enough for a compact car, at max, and whether there'd be any space to turn around back there was anybody's guess. You'd have to be really familiar with the place to venture into one of these lanes with a vehicle.

Fluorescents lit the first alleyway. Narrower than most, strictly a cut-through, it had a window but no door. He cut down the next access and headed to the back of the brown brick. Motion lights greeted him. Enough to light up a stadium. Or an interrogation room. The small lot behind her store was probably brighter now than it had been when the sun was in full-shine mode this afternoon.

Not that he blamed her—a pretty single woman living alone couldn't be too careful. Hell, inviting him over wasn't a brilliant move on her part, especially after he'd admitted to stalking her whereabouts via Google. Maybe he'd point that out.

He shook his head, sending snow flying. What the hell was up with him, getting all protective over a woman he'd just met?

He swept a glance at what was essentially her backyard. A small patch of asphalt, a couple of metal garbage cans strapped to the wall, a lamppost and what had to be her car. A tiny silver Hyundai. No scratches on the side that he could see. Guess she knew her way up and down that driveway. Hopefully she'd know her way up and down his body before he saw this parking lot again.

Blood pounded through his veins as he knocked on the door. Nerves? When was the last time he had those—high school? He'd been in assorted bands since college, and in assorted women since he'd joined his first band. The anticipation had adrenaline coursing through his system. Kind of like right before the stage lights came up. Only better.

He exhaled slowly, his breath forming a cloud against the cold. A little opening appeared in the miniblinds on the window. All he could see were fingertips, but he smiled anyway. Metal clinked and thunked on the other side of the door. More than one lock—smart. That's what he wanted, a woman with a brain to go with her—

"Beauty."

Standing in front of him, barefoot, a tiny dog tucked under her arm, Calli might as well have sucker-punched him. For such a small, innocent-looking woman, she packed a majorly sexy wallop.

"I've been thinking about how you looked this afternoon, but I forgot how beautiful you are." Thanks to her love of outdoor lighting, the full blush filling every pore of her face was his to enjoy.

"Think you have to butter me up to get past my guard dog?"

The *guard dog* was doing more shivering than snarling.

"He looks tough, but no." A minute might have passed, it could've been less, but the arctic wind made it feel like eternity.

Calli shifted foot-to-foot, her eyes roaming from his face to his feet. The dog shook some more—vigorously—

and Travis cupped his nearly numb hands to his face to blow on them. One of them had to make a move before they all turned into ice sculptures.

Apparently it was going to be him. "I can go, Calli."

Her eyes snapped to his face. "Don't—oh god, I'm standing here like a moron while you freeze your ass off. It's just, um, how did you know where I live?"

Hell, first shocking the shit out of her at the store, now this. Way to come across as a pervy stalker. Amazing she'd even opened the door for him. "Your sister told me, while we were at the coffee shop."

Calli's eyes widened, not quite as bulging as the Chihuahua's, but close. "You asked Caitlyn where I live?"

"No, nothing like that. Shit, I'm making this worse, aren't I?"

"Well..."

He had to smile. The way she cocked her head to the side, the little shrug. Damn, so cute. "She mentioned giving me a tour of the store. Said that the owner, who was also her sister, lived upstairs. Once I realized that Caitlyn wasn't my Scrabble girl, the pieces fit that her sister must be." His toes were officially numb, but he deserved it. "I should've told you all this before shutting down my computer and driving over here." And now, the part where he behaved like a decent guy, not Travis Graham, womanizing charmer of panties in three provinces and at least four states. "I'm going to head home. If you give me your number, we could talk, which I would very much like to do."

"I'd rather we, uh... "

The frigid November night had turned the tip of her nose red. The pink on her cheeks had nothing to do with the weather. Both were fucking adorable.

"Pick up our game online?" He sounded like a desperate man. Appropriate, because that's exactly how he felt.

"No, I want... Ugh, I'm not very experienced at this stuff."

"Me either." He laughed when she raised an eyebrow at him. "What—it's true." And it was—he'd never had to wait in subzero weather for an invitation from a woman.

"You're full of shit, but I'd like you to come in anyway. If you still want to... Travis."

"I want to." Jumped all over that, hadn't he? The sound of his name in her sexy voice, the way she tested it on those pretty lips, heated the blood now surging through his veins. He stepped inside and she triple-bolted the door behind him. Locking him in with her—fine by him. "I like it when you say my name."

She smiled up at him while returning her dog to the ground. "I like it too. I mean, when you call me Calli."

"It suits you. Very feminine, with a hint of incredibly cute." He shrugged his coat off and delivered it to her waiting arms. Watching her move around, the simple act of hanging a coat on a hook, had him itching to touch her. She caught him staring. Smiled a little, blushed a lot. Damn.

Her hands knotted together in front of her waist. "Would you like to come upstairs?"

So sweet, so proper. So unlike the women he'd grown

accustomed to. If they were chatting online, he'd play on her words, tell her it didn't matter where he came, as long as it was with her.

For now, he dialed it back. "Very much. Lead the way." He kept his hands at his sides as they climbed the wooden stairs. Took all his willpower, but he didn't touch her. Just stared at her pert ass swaying in front of his face. His cock pushed against his fly. Taking the edge off a few hours ago didn't count for much now, not with Calli's bare legs mere inches away, tempting him to the point of insanity.

"You don't have a heart condition or something, do you?" she asked when they entered her apartment at the top of the stairs.

"Nope. All my organs have been tested and checked as clean."

Again with the shy smile. "Just out of shape, then?"

"I like to think I'm not. I run ten kilometers without stopping and hit the gym at least three times a week." To hell with it, he was going for it. He stepped closer and lightly cupped her waist. "Decide for yourself... put your hands on my stomach, or chest, or whatever else you want to check the fitness of."

The top of her head barely reached his chin. She looked up at him through those long, dark lashes. Reached out tentatively and placed one palm on his chest. The second one landed a bit lower, sending a streak of heat straight to his groin.

"See, you're doing it again."

"What's that, sweetheart?"

"Kind of huffing and puffing." She caught her lip

between her teeth and worried it. Big blue-gray eyes looked up at him.

Was she truly unaware that she was the reason for his short breaths? "That's on you, Calli. It's been a while since a woman has wound me this tight." Wrong thing to say, since it caused her to pull back, stripping him of their contact.

"I don't get it." Her arms crisscrossed over her chest in a hug. She shook her head and put more space between them by stepping around the furniture in her living room. "Want something—to drink, I mean?"

One step forward and two back. No problem. He'd dance with her all night, as long as she didn't kick him out again. "That'd be great. Whatever you've got." He followed her through an arch that separated the living room from the kitchen area, then leaned on the counter beside her as she poured two glasses of cranberry juice. He let his fingers linger over hers as she passed him one of the purple highballs. "What don't you get?"

"You—being interested in me."

"Because we met playing Scrabble?"

No answer, she just shook her head again. "So, do you want to... sit, or..." Her eyes darted from the dinette set to the couch to a darkened hallway. "I mean, I know you came over to... do stuff."

They'd gone from hot and heavy online to having an elephant between them now that they were sharing air instead of cyberspace. And she thought he only wanted sex—worse, she thought he expected it. No good.

"Do you have my Scrabble board?"

"Yes. In the living room."

"Let's go in there and play."

"Scrabble?"

"Yeah." For starters. He nodded for her to lead the way, then followed close behind. "But with a twist. Truth or Dare Scrabble." She stopped abruptly, half-spinning to face him. Pure, automatic reflexes saved her white blouse from his juice. The floor didn't get so lucky. "Shit. Sorry."

"You can get a ticket for following too close, you know." Her tone was scolding, but her lips had curved into a playful smile he could easily get addicted to.

"I'll clean it up, officer."

"You set up the board. I'll take care of the spill."

Luck had been on his side when he found the vintage portable Scrabble game in a pawn shop. His full-size board wouldn't have fit in his pocket. But this thing had seen better days. "I'm not sure if all the tiles are here."

"You could count them."

Or he could stare at the hem of her skirt lifting higher up her smooth, taut hamstrings as she rubbed a cloth over the hardwood in a circular motion. He'd never heard of houndstooth before tonight, but he certainly had a new appreciation for it.

She peeked over her shoulder—probably because he hadn't answered—and caught him ogling her backside. "So? How's the situation?"

"Pretty fantastic."

"The game," she said, mock-scolding again. She

repositioned from all-fours to her knees, ass resting on her heels with her hands folded in her lap. "Do we have all the stuff we need to play?"

Hell yes, they did. "I think we'll be good." Very good.

She arched her back slightly in a stretch. "Then I'll put this away and be right back."

Give him strength, because he was sure going to need it once the game started. He set things up on the coffee table. Not good enough. He'd be able to see her through the glass top and iron frame, but she'd still be too far away. He scanned the room for something he could use to support the board and came up with a wide, hardcover book about stones. That'd do. By the time she came from the kitchen, he had their game waiting on the middle cushion of the couch. Close enough to touch her if the opportunity arose and give him a full view even if it didn't.

"Here." She handed him a fresh glass of juice. This one had a straw. A pink one—the bendy kind. Exactly right for her.

"Thanks. This is a nice little apartment."

"Little being the operative word."

"It's not bad. Looks about the same as mine." From what he could see, the place was compact, but not cramped or claustrophobic. Where his was stark white with only the basic, necessary items, hers was cozy and warm, with cream-colored walls and furniture, pinks and purples adding color to everything from pillows and pictures to the cup in his hand. The place reminded him of her—feminine but not overdone. Natural in the best ways.

She dragged a donut-shaped doggie bed from the corner. "Charming, come. No, not on the couch, on your bed."

The tiny dog that'd been at her heels since she'd set him down obeyed, but he didn't look thrilled about it. Maybe it was the name as much as being relegated to the floor. Not exactly the coolest tag at the dog park.

"Your dog's name is Charming?"

"Technically, it's Prince Charming."

Poor dog. No wonder he was doing the canine version of a scowl. "I don't think he likes you telling me his secrets."

"The curled-lip thing? Ignore it, he's all show. He's not used to visitors. Or strangers. Or men in general."

Mental note—bring dog treats next time. Also noted, Calli's relationship habits. She probably got a lot of offers, but from the sound of it, she didn't give out many invites to her personal space. More reason not to screw up the one he had.

"Ready to play?" he asked after she settled onto the couch across from him.

The way she'd arranged her legs beneath her created a tunnel up the middle. With the short skirt riding up toward her hips, that opening afforded him the tiniest hint of pink. Panties that she'd had her hand inside not so long ago. *It's wet in my panties...* her exact words.

He forced his eyes up, following the line of buttons he very much wanted to rip off with his teeth so he could see the treasures contained in her polka-dot bra. By the time he got to her face, her cheeks were pretty pink.

Either she read minds or he'd left his mask at home.

She picked up the vinyl bag with the tiles and shook it. "Should we pull tiles to see who goes first?"

"Not necessary. I'm a firm believer in ladies first, for everything." He wouldn't have thought the color of her skin could go much deeper pink, but it did. Delicate fingers toyed with the buttons near her tits, the glossy dark-purple tips against the white taunting him, whether she intended it or not. "Nice nails."

"They're sort of extreme, I know. I'm not really a makeup kind of girl, but I love loud nail polish."

"It suits you—the nail polish is sexy. As for makeup, you don't need it."

"You're quite the flatterer."

If she only knew how wrong she was. He'd been less than kind on more occasions than he'd like to count. "No, I'm just getting warmed up for our game. All truth from here out, Calli."

She blinked rapidly while fiddling with the tiles on her rack. "I've never heard of Truth or Dare Scrabble. How do you play?"

Time for some quick thinking to back up his suggestion. Rules that'd help him get to know her... and get past those damn buttons. "Same as regular Scrabble, but after we each make a play, the person with the lower scoring word has to answer a truth or dare."

"Dictionary or no?"

"If you need one, sure."

She laughed, full out. More than the little giggle that'd

escaped while they were in her store earlier. That had been cute. The low, mildly husky quality of her voice carried into this laugh, and it was anything but cute—it was make-your-cock-ache sexy.

"I don't need a book to beat you." Something that looked suspiciously like smugness slid across her face. "You aren't one of those sore-loser types, are you?"

Whether they ended up naked or not, this was going to be fun.

Chapter Nine

"Make your move, sweetheart."

He'd called her that online, and earlier too. Hearing it in his deep voice, having his eyes on her and seeing his lips form the most incredible smile while he called her *sweetheart*... gah. If she had a speck of courage, she'd forfeit the game and jump into his lap. That's what her sister would do. What any normal woman would do.

So it was truth or dare time. She'd played with her friends a few times back in the middle-school grades. Questions about the boys they liked, if they ever put tissue in their bras, stuff like that. They'd dared each other to phone their crushes and say silly things. Easy stuff, compared to what this game would be like. But she couldn't wait. This was a game she couldn't lose, regardless of the score.

"*Block*, double-letter score for the K and a double-word score... thirty-six points." She looked up at him while digging into the bag for replacement tiles. "Aren't you going to write it down?"

He smiled and jotted the number under her initial. "You've got a competitive streak, don't you?"

"If you want me to answer that, it'll cost you a word

worth at least thirty-seven points."

"*When* I beat you this round, that won't be my question."

"Good luck with that." Calli could list the amount of things she felt confident about on one hand. Her Scrabble skills were on that list. Thousands of hours playing against a computer instead of having real social connections didn't seem like such a waste now. Using her nerdiness against Travis—only the most attractive man she'd ever been within handling range of—brought out a cocky side she didn't know she possessed. By the huge smile on his face, she guessed he didn't mind it. Good, because she kind of liked it too.

Travis draped one arm over the back of her couch. The long-sleeved indigo t-shirt hugged his forearm, shoulder and biceps. Solid, all of it, with two very nice, very hard balls of muscle.

Thank god he had his eyes fixed on the game, because ogling him while thinking about the words *hard* and *balls* made her nipples tighten. Shifting position didn't help. In fact, the satin buffing those hard peaks shot an arrow of need straight between her legs. Trying to get comfortable in the short skirt was bad enough. No way could she adjust in any way that'd give her some…relief. At least her situation wasn't obvious. By his incessant tapping of a tile against the game board, it appeared he was clueless about her situation. *Tap, tap, tap.* Pause. *Tap, tap, tap.*

"Don't worry, I'll go easy on you the first time around." Holy god, who was this woman talking, because it sure wasn't her. Whatever had possessed her, it wasn't letting go, either. "I'll ask you a nice, safe question."

His eyes flicked upward. "Yeah?" Pure mischief there.

"I don't have the same plan for you." Methodically, he placed his tiles, making eye contact between each one. P, R, I, then a skip over the existing C, blank tile, L, E. "The blank is a—"

"K." Oh boy.

"It is. *Prickle*, spanning two double-word scores, is forty points." *Tap, tap, tap,* went the last tile in his hand. Then he laid it on the board. "But *prickled* is worth forty-eight and it's also a bingo."

Oh shit.

"For ninety-eight points. And the rules state," he jotted his score under his initial, "that a bingo gets me a truth *and* a dare."

She huffed and crossed her arms. "You didn't tell me that before my turn."

"So you had a bingo, but you chose not to play it?" His hand dipped into the bag for seven new tiles. "Now you know for next time."

"Not fair, Travis."

"You're incredibly cute when you pout." He leaned forward, over the board, and touched her knee oh-so-lightly. "But you've got the sexiest voice I've ever heard—say my name again."

He had to be able to hear her heart as it galloped up her throat. She swallowed to keep it from leaping from her mouth when she spoke. "Is that your dare?" Did she want him to say yes or no... even she didn't know.

"No, sweetheart, you don't get off that easily."

One big whoop popped out of her mouth. "Sorry,

occupational hazard of working in a store that sells sexy accessories—everything starts to sound dirty, and you said—"

"Get off." His thumb stroked the crease of her folded leg. Back and forth, dipping into the crevice the tiniest bit. Her body didn't miss the hint. It took conscious effort not to open her legs wider and invite him to tickle another, better crevice.

"Truth or dare, Calli?"

"I-I thought I had to do both."

"You do. But I'll let you choose the order."

"Dare."

The movement on her leg stopped. "I thought you'd pick truth."

"You thought wrong... Travis." The heat in his stare caused her to stumble over her words, stretching the two syllables of his name into a long whisper. She might as well have said *fuck me now*. He'd have to be an idiot not to know that's what she was thinking. And Travis was most definitely not an idiot.

"Take off your skirt."

Holy shit. Her eyes hurt, they bugged out of her head so far. "Don't I get a warm-up dare first? Something... easier?"

"I would've told you to take off your stockings, but you beat me to it. Your heels too. You didn't leave me a lot of options."

"Can we negotiate?" The way he'd been staring at her chest, she'd expected the top to go first. That wouldn't be such a big deal—a bra wasn't much different from a bikini top, right? "How about my blouse instead?"

"No, the pretty shirt stays on for now." Eyes bright with obvious desire worked their way up, as if he was mentally unbuttoning each and every tiny pearl. "But I am willing to make a deal. You can keep the skirt."

"If you don't want the blouse and you're letting me keep the skirt, what do you want? For me to…do something?" Because if he ordered her to her knees, she'd be on them in a second.

His head shook slightly as a sly smile stretched across his face. "Not yet. But I am looking forward to seeing you dance."

"Oh no. I don't dance. Not in front of people." The thought of dancing in front of another human being filled her stomach with a thousand flitting butterflies.

"Then you'd better not lose too many rounds. You dancing for me is staying on my dare list, Calli. I'm just not sure if I want you dressed or naked when you do it."

Oh dear god. Daring her to suck his cock or bend over the couch—those things she might be able to handle. Wanted to handle. If he made her dance, or sing, she might keel over. This date would end with Travis watching her hyperventilate, not gyrate. "I can't dance, Travis. I really can't."

The devil disappeared from his expression. He moved from his end of the couch to crouch on the floor at her hip. His hands slid over her—one on her bare leg, the other on the small of her back. Even through the cotton, her skin electrified under his palm.

"Like I said in my message earlier—I'll only do things that you want. That includes the dares. If you take them, it won't be because you have to—it'll be because you want to."

"I tell you I can't dance and you think I'll *want* to dance for you before the end of one Scrabble game?"

The hand on her back traced up her spine and sifted through her hair. Sparks exploded everywhere he touched. This kind of contact was probably normal for him and meant nothing. Not for her. Not at all. It'd been so long since fingers other than her own had caressed her skin, she'd forgotten how intoxicating it could be.

He pushed off his haunches, positioning himself very close to her face. Close enough to feel his breath mingle with hers. Close enough to kiss her—only he didn't.

"I'm looking forward to finding out. As for this round, the price for keeping your skirt is your panties."

"I accept your terms." She stood—though he didn't give her much space to do so—and snaked her fingers up, under her skirt. Actually, removing her underwear in this manner proved more difficult than she expected. A thong would've been relatively simple. Reach, hook, yank. The boy-cut shorts covered a lot more ground, and they clung to her body like skin. And the damn skirt was ultra-close fitting. To get at the undies, she'd practically have to shove the skirt up over her hips. Maintaining an element of mystery—or modesty—would be next to impossible.

Travis was clearly enjoying the entire process. Hands stuffed into his jeans' pockets and sporting an exceptional grin, he continued to crowd her, never taking his eyes off her. She ought to be furious or humiliated. Instead her breasts were tingly, her clit was on high alert and the heat between her legs ensured that the panties giving her so much trouble were beyond damp. She'd never get them off this way.

"Troubles?"

"It's this skirt."

"The houndstooth one. It's different. I like it."

"It's also too tight for me to take off my panties without showing you my stuff."

"Good thing I don't mind if you do."

"Travis, come on."

The amusement slipped away, replaced by a much hungrier smile. "Be more specific, sweetheart, especially when you're teasing me by saying my name in that sexy voice."

She'd been so upset when the doctors told her the damage to her throat was irreparable. But Travis liked her low, gravelly tone. Huh. At least one good thing had come from the attack.

"Come on and what?" he asked while getting closer, though that hardly seemed possible.

"Turn around." She swallowed, trying to banish the wobble from her voice. "You dared me to give you my panties...you never said I had to take them off in front of you."

"You're right." He gave her his back, but no extra space. "Next time I'll be more specific."

Quick as she could, she wrestled the polka-dot panties from her body, then tugged the skirt back into place. Now that she had them, what was she supposed to do with them? Start a pile that would hopefully have some of his clothes in it before too long? She wasn't about to hand them over—they were practically soaked through at the crotch, for god's sake. A quick show that she'd paid his price, then she'd tuck them into the couch cushions.

"Done…see?" She snapped them to his right side before he turned around. Wrong move. Apparently Travis was a righty—one with great reflexes. The panties now belonged to him. "Don't—oh god, you can't keep them, they're—" Soaked with her juices, for gods' sake.

The panties went up, over her head, until they hung from his extended arm like a flag from a flagpole. She jumped for them, to no avail. She was short, he was tall. 'Nuff said.

"Relax. It's like checkers or chess. I hold on to the pieces you lose until the game's over, that's all." The panties made a slow descent. Travis's eyes stayed on hers as he tracked the tiny garment into his back pocket.

At least he hadn't commented on—

"You weren't lying about them being hot. Or wet."

Her face burned with the heat of an August day and no sunscreen. "Now you know," she said, enjoying the rise of his eyebrows at her intentionally misleading statement. "I don't lie."

After torturing her by ensuring that the goods in his pocket were secure, Travis returned to his end of the couch. "Ready for your question?"

"If I answer that, your turn will be over."

"Then thanks for not answering."

Settling into her spot took work. And a lot of adjusting. Not only was the skirt *not* cooperating in her quest to conceal her cootchie, it seemed determined to climb higher up her thighs than before. "I should've given you this damn skirt."

"Maybe next round."

"You wouldn't..." Leave her naked from the waist down—she bet he might. "Question please. I have a move to make and a round to win."

"Why isn't your dog used to visitors, strangers or men in general?" The question had Calli squirming as much as trying to shimmy panties from underneath her curve-hugging skirt had. Meaning it was a good one to ask. Sure, he'd been tempted to ask her a racier question—something about which of the store's sex toys she preferred or how often she used them. This was better. Plus, it kept her off-balance, swinging between hot and serious. And she was damn cute when she was thinking. Her pretty face and hot body would've been enough to turn him on. The fact that she had a quick wit and functioning brain made her irresistible.

"I don't go out much."

"That's it?"

She kept her eyes on her tiles, moving them around on the rack. "I answered your question."

"Five words isn't much of an answer."

"You didn't tell me there was a minimum word requirement. You really should've been more *specific*."

Damn, she had him again. Hung by his own comments.

She looked up at him, a hint of naughty in those big eyes. "You can buy more words... if you want to."

Changing the game on him—he liked it. "What'll it cost me, and for how many?" The wheels turned as she perused him. Her eyes might as well have been her hands, because the effect was the same. Not that he hadn't been ogled before. It used to be a turn-on, knowing women wanted him, but it'd lost its novelty. Under Calli's openly appreciative gaze, though, his skin heated and his cock swelled. God help him if she asked for his pants.

"Three complete sentences for your shirt."

"Deal. Sentences first."

"No way. I need inspiration."

Spunky and not a total pushover. He liked her more by the second. "Bare skin for a bare soul?"

"Exactly."

"I hope tattoos don't offend you." His heart notched up as he peeled the t-shirt over his head. He'd never given it a moment's consideration before, that a woman might take issue with his ink. This was different. Calli was different. She'd flirted with him sight unseen, based on messages, not because he was on a stage. He'd wanted that—to be seen as more than a conquest for the night, a tick off somebody's bucket list that included *bang a musician.*

"Wow, you have a lot. With your clothes on, I never would've guessed." Not exactly an endorsement, but she hadn't turned away, either.

"It started with one shoulder and went from there over the years. I'd never get one that couldn't be covered, though, for professional reasons."

"Why wouldn't you want everybody to see them... they're part of the whole 'sexy rocker' vibe, aren't they?"

"You're asking a lot of questions for somebody who's supposed to be answering mine." Not that he minded. And the shy smile on her face while she continued checking him out—he didn't mind that, either. "I got my first tattoo long before anybody paid me to play a guitar. Also, I keep my clothes on while I'm on stage."

"That's unfortunate for your female fans."

"I guess that means you like tattoos." When was the last time he'd fished for a compliment—five years ago, ten?

"Not necessarily... but I like yours."

Damn and double damn. Her voice already did it for him, but when she spoke quietly like that, the soft-husky combo completely lit his fuse. The muscles in his arms twitched. He wanted to knock the game board out of the way and drag her on top of him. Feel her hands on his skin as she explored every line on his arms, shoulders, chest.

He swallowed hard. "You still owe me three sentences."

"All right." She fidgeted again. "You met my sister, saw how she is—gorgeous and exciting and outgoing. I'm the opposite. She's like this beacon that draws everybody's attention, whereas I'm more comfortable being the lighthouse keeper. I guess you could say I'm a homebody and leave it at that."

Whoa. The subtext in her statements told him she stayed home for reasons other than loving her apartment. "How much older is your sister?"

She cocked her head. "I'm older. Not by much, eleven months. Irish twins, as they say."

That explained a few things. Why she and her sister were close, which he'd picked up from his conversation with Caitlyn. Why Calli would feel the need to compare them. Growing up with a sister so close in age would've fostered a lot of competition, in all areas, he'd bet. Thinking the other girl had her beat, though—not in his books.

"Technically, I shouldn't have answered that question." She turned her attention to their game, scowling as she shuffled tiles in her rack. "Double-word score on *fop* and *do*…twenty-seven measly points." The scowl turned on him. "Don't even think about playing another bingo on this board, mister."

"Master, not mister." He had to smile when she rolled her eyes at him. All his luck had disappeared after the first move. She'd win this round. And he didn't mind one bit. "*Hae* for eighteen. Ladies' choice."

She clapped with genuine enthusiasm, the little bounce that went with it making her tits jiggle and her skirt inch closer to her hips. Holy mother, another celebration like that and he'd have one hell of a view. He'd never been one to throw a game of any kind, but there was a first time for everything.

On his side of the board, he didn't have much to lose. Jeans, boxers, socks, a belt. If she asked for jeans he wasn't putting the belt back on, so it'd be gone too.

She leaned forward, making a big show of deciding. "Hmm... what to choose... "

The move pressed her tits against the fabric. That'd be his next move—getting those damn buttons out of the way.

"I'm inclined to dare you, just for payback, but I do have questions." Her tongue slid across her bottom lip. "Nope. Questions will have to wait. I'm definitely going with dare."

"What'll it be? Socks, belt, one-hundred push-ups, sing you a song...?" Or pants, so she could see the evidence of how exciting he found her, despite what she thought about herself.

"You sing?"

"Sometimes."

"What kind of songs? Covers, or do you write your own?"

"You changing your mind, sweetheart? Truth instead of dare?"

She crossed her arms over her chest. "You wish. Jeans, please."

This would make things interesting. He reversed the thick strip of black leather through the buckle, then worked the metal button. She watched every action, big eyes even wider, as though she'd never seen a man take off his clothes before. As if she were starving and he was dinner, dessert and a midnight snack all rolled into one. His cock liked it. He liked it. More than was wise for the moment.

He paused with his hand on the zipper. "What if I'm commando under here? You might get more than you bargained for."

"As long as you're not wearing a man-thong," she waggled her fingers at him, "carry on."

Ready or not. He hooked his fingers under the edge and shoved, cursing under his breath when manual adjustments were needed to free his obvious bulge from the opening.

"Troubles?" she asked, then giggled.

"If you're offering to help, then yes."

She held out one hand after he yanked the second leg free. "I'll take those." First thing she did was fold them into a neat little square. Second thing was to yank her panties from the pocket. "And I'll take these, thank you very much."

"Conniving wench." Served him right for thinking with his dick.

She treated him to a smug smile. "My turn." No glaring at her pieces this time. No focus at all, in fact. Seconds ticked into minutes, half that time spent with Calli's eyes flitting across the board—at him. The flush on her cheeks deepened and spread into the neckline of her shirt. And if she licked her lips one more time while eyeing him squarely in the hard-on zone, he was going to have to jump her. Immediately.

"My tiles suck."

He groaned. Suck was not a word he could handle

from her lips right now. "Swap 'em... if you don't mind losing again."

"No, I have a word. It's a little one, even though they can actually be quite large and immensely satisfying. Double-letter score on the D, for a total of seven points."

Now that he hadn't expected. "You made *dildo*."

"Good reading."

"And you opened up the triple-word square."

"Oh, did I?" Purple nails mock-covered her lips. "Oops."

She'd been too embarrassed to take off her skirt, yet now she was handing him a win. Interesting game—and woman. He placed his tiles. D, I, C, blank.

"*Dice* for eighteen. Too bad you had to use another blank."

"I didn't." He flashed an E from his rack. "It's *dick*, not *dice*. And I guarantee it's better than your dildo."

"Nearly three times better, according to the score."

"At least three times better, even on a bad day." Extra blood raced to his cock, causing it to throb and strain against his boxers. Whether it'd been noticeable or not, Calli's eyes had moved to his crotch. And again with the lips and tongue. He ground out, "Truth or dare?" and prayed she didn't quit her current bold streak.

"Dare," she whispered.

So maybe there really was a god. "I want those buttons undone." Her hands moved to the top one. *Pop.* Lower, to the second. *Pop.* Then the third, never taking her eyes from him as she pushed it through the hole. *Pop.* "Stop. I want to do the rest."

"O-okay. Should I c—"

"Stay there." As much as he wanted her on her knees in front of him, he didn't let her finish the offer. That'd be the end of his thinly held control. He moved to her side of the couch. "Face me." Good god damn, those eyes staring up at him. At his face, at his cock jutting forward in the boxer briefs. Still too tempting. He knelt, his body bumping her thighs apart as he shuffled closer. With no resistance.

She gasped when the skirt rode straight up to her hips, then grabbed the edge of the fabric, attempting to hold it in place. Too late. Heat from her core taunted his chest, daring him to press tight against her. Not yet. He needed those inches of separation a few minutes longer.

"This is a pretty shirt." He cupped her hands with his. That touch, having her small, soft hands inside his, jolted him. He moved them from the buttons and deposited them flat on his chest. Instant fire. And when her delicate fingers wandered over his chest and stomach, it spread like brushfire over every inch of his skin. "Tell me I don't have to win another round before I can kiss you."

"I'll put it on your account."

He brushed his lips across hers. "I'll take that deal." The way she tipped her head, opened for him, was innocence and sensuality—a heady combination. He stroked into her mouth with his tongue. Pulled back until their mouths met with the barest, softest touch. He lingered there, fighting the urge to plunder as she wiggled closer. And closer. Close enough for her fingers to reach the thin screen of material covering his cock.

"Calli." He didn't know what to ask for. For her to stop stroking him, or keep stroking him, or more.

Her hand slid inside his boxers and circled him. "Yes."

Fuck the buttons. "Put this on my account too." He grabbed the open edges and yanked. The crisp tear of cotton and scramble of plastic pearls startled her—and her dog, now standing by Travis's hip and growling pretty damn loud for a pocket-sized canine. "He's not going to bite me in the ass, is he?"

Calli turned her head toward the little beast. "I don't know. He's never seen me kissing or…anything. I haven't had a man over since I got him."

"How long have you had him?"

"If I answer, it'll count as a truth. Your tab is getting pretty full."

His cock jerked in her hand—its way of letting her know that his tab wasn't the only thing that was going to get full. "Bill me."

"Almost two years."

"But you've dated, you've—"

"No. Nothing."

"Seriously?" he asked, watching pink flood her cheeks as she nodded. He hated to ask more, especially now, but it made no sense—a beautiful, smart woman going without for so long. He'd walk away if he had to. "Any reason for the celibacy that I should know about?"

"No, god no. Nothing like that. I've never even had a cold sore."

Another thank you went up to the clouds. Since Calli's hand was still wrapped around his cock, stroking him with agonizing lightness, he'd take his chances with Prince Charming's teeth. "You're driving me crazy, touching me like that."

She released him like a hot potato. "Sorry...I don't have tons of experience with the male equipment."

"Not bad crazy." He guided her hand back to his cock, closed her fingers around it again. "Does it feel like my equipment is complaining?" He sucked in a breath as she gripped him tighter and slid her palm up and down his length.

"Actually, it feels a little angry. All that pulsing and jerking while I'm petting it so nicely."

He laughed, then caught her mouth in another kiss. From sexy to shy to sexy again. As much as wanted to bury himself inside her, if they played like this all night and nothing more, he'd go home smiling.

She pulled back from the kiss, slightly out of breath and completely glassy-eyed. "You took care of my buttons, I guess it's time for us to make another move."

"I haven't finished with your buttons yet, sweetheart. Not by a longshot. I want them all undone." He nuzzled her cleavage while sliding the shirt from her shoulders, down her arms and off. "Your skin is so damn soft. And so fair."

"That's a nice way of saying I'm pale."

"That's me trying to take it slow and gentlemanly, when the truth is, I want to tell you you're beautiful and sexy and fucking irresistible. Your skin is perfect. Warm, silky, creamy. And it tastes sweet. So sweet I want to sample every inch, starting here…" He nudged one breast free of the bra and licked it from the luscious swell to the hard, raspberry-colored tip. He slid one hand along the hot, smooth skin of her thigh. Higher, to the velvety folds between her legs, where he stroked until *he* couldn't take any more. "And here…" He jiggled one finger against her clit, groaning around her nipple when her hips jerked forward for more.

A shrill bark sounded beside him, followed by a low, guttural wail. Man's best friend did not look pleased.

"Bedroom—it has a door."

"Hold tight." He scooped her into his arms. She was a tiny thing, light and warm. He could carry her for hours. Especially with her tits pressed against his chest and her pussy riding the desperate ridge in his boxers. So maybe not hours.

Her mouth went to work on his neck. Choppy breaths filled his ear. Then a little moan as she dug her heels into his back and ground against him. Holy hell, if she came now, he was done for. "Wait for me, sweetheart. I want to be the one to make you come."

"You are."

"With my mouth," he said, chuckling as the grinding came to an immediate halt. He closed the door in her dog's face and pinned her against the back of it. "Where's the light switch?"

"Don't have one. Just a table lamp by the bed, to your left."

Three steps in his knee connected with a dresser. "Shit." Practically tripped over a stool next. "It's pitch black in here."

"Sorry. Put me down and I'll get the light."

"No." He cradled her ass closer when she tried to shimmy free. "Fuck." Stubbed toe from what had to be the leg of the bed. He put a hand down and felt around for the top. "We're there. Now you can get it."

He'd made it a policy to do his fucking at the woman's place, never his own. Easier that way. Tidier all around. But while women's bedrooms could be interesting, incredible dens of femininity, coziness or exotic sensuality, sometimes they turned out to be scary places. Some he wished he could un-remember. A couple he'd been lucky to escape with his dick intact.

He held his breath while the lamp switch clicked. Then it was all good.

She turned on her hands and knees to find Travis smiling at her. Not the sexy I-want-to-eat-you-up smile from their hot and heavy make-out session in the living room. More of a you're-so-cute smile. Didn't quite go with the solid erection filling in his boxers. At least he still had that.

"What?"

"Just appreciating the view... of you... and your room."

She glanced around, trying to see it through his eyes, then groaned. White-and-purple striped wallpaper, fancy pillows, a zillion candles and more than a few stuffed animals. More of a little girl's bedroom than an entrepreneurial woman who ran a sexy store. And then there was her. A quick peek down and she groaned again. A sexpot she was not. Boobs flopping out the top of her bra, skirt bunched around her waist.

"Not exactly an advertisement for a romance store, huh?"

"You look pretty perfect to me." It sounded good. Too good. The words came through lips that'd kissed god knows how many women.

She didn't blame any of those women. Heck, she was about to become one of them. And why not, look at him. From his dark hair, soulful hazel eyes and sinful lips to his hard, cut body sporting dark tattoos from wrists to collarbone—Travis was the poster boy for sexy. Add his brain, charm and musician status into the mix and jumping into bed with him was more automatic than breathing. He could say anything he wanted and get away with it. But to tell *her* that she looked perfect or beautiful or sexy...just knocked it home that he was here for one reason. And her personality wasn't it.

So what. One night with Travis would be better than anything she'd ever done, regardless of his reasons for settling. No more analysis or worrying, just fun. She could do fun for one night. Serious and steady would be waiting for her in the morning, same as always.

"I grabbed protection from downstairs before you got here—it's on the dresser you slammed into."

He didn't give it a glance. "Don't need it."

"Uh, yeah, we do." She sat up, tugged her skirt enough to cover the basics and crossed her arms over her freewheeling boobs. "I'm not on the Pill, obviously, since I haven't had sex in...a while...and you've probably been with, I don't know...hundreds of women. Probably so many you've lost count."

"I meant we don't need it *yet*." The bed shifted under his weight as he sat, then propped on one arm alongside her. "I want to be with you, Calli. You. Very much, as you felt for yourself. But I'd rather go back in the living room and play a purely innocent game of Scrabble with you than do anything we need a condom for. Not if you don't want it and not while you're upset."

No promises to make her feel good or guilt trips for getting cold feet. Shame on her for sticking him in the jerk column because of his looks and his profession. Now she'd killed the mood like a skunk under a Mac truck. "I won't make a dumb scene if you want to leave."

"Did I say I want to leave?"

"No."

"Do you want me to leave?"

"No."

"Good," he said, reaching up to tug a chunk of her dangling hair.

If she was going for it, time to do it right—right now. She backed off the bed, unhooked her bra and let it fall away. The skirt followed. She wiggled it to the floor, leaving her wholly exposed to a man who'd probably been with ten-out-of-tens on a regular basis. God, give her the strength not to dive under the bed.

"You have an incredible body."

"I'm sure you've seen—" She bit her tongue before *better* slipped out. "Thank you."

Anatomy didn't lie, and Travis's boxers still contained evidence that she turned him on. Go figure. His eyes roamed her naked body, heating her skin, drawing her nipples to taut peaks, making her slick between the legs. She twined her fingers together and fidgeted. For all the thousands of romantic books and movies she'd devoured, she didn't have a clue what to do next. What little sex she'd had fell into the on-her-back-in-the-dark category. It had started fast and ended fast. None of this drawn-out seduction stuff.

Travis shifted to a half-sit and reached for her hand. "Sweetheart, we can save this for another day. Let's go play some Scrabble—regular, pedestrian rules."

Oh no. If she let him walk out of her bedroom now, that'd be it. She steeled herself with a deep breath and moved to the bed. With a light shove, she pushed Travis to his back and straddled him. "I'm sick of going backward."

Chapter Six

"Forward it is. Or any other direction you like—upward, downward, sideways..." Subtle movements accompanied his offer, all of them bringing his jersey-covered erection in contact with her clit.

"I'm sorry for saying those bitchy things before." Goose bumps populated her skin en masse as his hands skated over her hips, up her stomach, breasts and neck to her face. "I'm just nervous. I've never done anything like...well, like any of this. But I want to."

A smile ticked on his lips. "Picking up a guy online on your bucket list, is it?"

"No—god no."

"Having sex with a stranger?"

"I'm not that kind of girl," she said, and he cocked an eyebrow at her. "We're not total strangers...otherwise I wouldn't know about your cat."

"True." His fingers worked their way back down, stopping at her breasts. He cupped them, stroked them, circled his thumbs over her nipples. "What else do you know that proves we're not strangers?"

"I know your name. Your job."

"Think so?"

"Travis Graham. Bassist for Black Box." She'd Googled his band after he and Caitlyn had left the store yesterday. Read his bio and ogled his headshots. That didn't count as honestly knowing him, of course, but it gave her some ammo to win his little challenge. "You've played all over Ontario, Québec, Michigan, Ohio and New York. You haven't been signed to a label yet, but you have a few original indie songs on iTunes."

"Hot, naked Wikipedia—I like it, but you're incorrect about that being my job. Playing guitar doesn't pay my rent." He tweaked her nipples hard enough to send a pain-pleasure streak straight to her core. Before she could grind her needy body onto him, he rolled her to her back, holding himself out of contact range. "Maybe it's not sex with a stranger you want...it's sex with a guy from a band."

The words were playful enough, but his voice had taken on an edge. A shadow had fallen over his face, one that had nothing to do with the low lighting in her dinky bedroom.

Her heart raced as she stared up at him. All the months she'd hidden in this apartment, protecting herself from any possible danger...now she'd possibly invited it into her bedroom. Stripped naked for a man she truly did not know. He could do a lot worse than her mugger had. She just didn't believe he would.

"It's not the band thing or the stranger thing," she whispered. "It's the way you use words. That's what first turned me on about you." Her pulse pounded, so loud he had to hear it as he stared down at her. "The fact that you're also ridiculously hot is like—bonus points."

The darkness receded, replaced by a smile that took her breath away. "You're saying I'm like the Q on a triple-letter square?"

"Better. The Q on a triple-letter square, played in both directions, in a seven-letter word for a bingo."

"That's a hell of a lot of points." His head lowered. Lips connected with her shoulder and blazed a trail of kisses up her neck, along her jaw to the dip below her mouth. "I'll do my best to earn every one of them."

Travis's bottom lip brushed hers. Soft and slow, teasing. Inviting her to open for him. She arched into him, sighing when he met her with the length of his body. His tongue slid along the seam of her lips, then dipped inside, torturing her with its delicious in and out motion. This is what the hype was about. Why people steamed car windows or got caught in indecent situations. A girl could lose all reason while being kissed like this, forget that she was plain and boring. With Travis's mouth on her, Calli was alive. A sex goddess, ready and wanting everything he offered.

Hands in his hair, legs around his waist, she pulled him down. He moved against her in a long, slow grind. Each pass deeper than the last. He dragged his hard length up her slit, across her clit, pushing her closer to the edge. Oh god, she wanted to come—wanted it so bad her clit throbbed.

Travis pulled his lips away and a low moan escaped. Hers. Low and brazen, it filled the room, and she sucked in a breath at the sound of it.

"Oh god, I-I didn't mean to be so...noisy. Kiss me again."

"If I swallow any more of those sexy noises of yours, I'm going to come before you do." He thrust along her again, adding a swivel at the top that took her closer to finishing.

She was getting to *him*? Wow.

He rolled their bodies again, positioning her squarely on top of his jersey-sheathed cock. He gripped her hips and urged her into a circular grind as he tilted into her. Once she'd joined in the rhythm, his hands moved to her breasts. "Stop fighting it and let me earn some of those damn points."

Blunted fingernails scraped her nipples. She shivered and moaned, eliciting a ragged curse from Travis.

"Bite me..." Her request barely made it out as a whisper. He groaned in reply, taking one diamond-hard nipple between his teeth.

"Oh god, that's so...more, please, Travis..." Heat bloomed beneath his mouth as he nipped and laved—one nipple, then the other. She arched, her body making an S as she sought more pressure for both her nipples and clit.

A growl rumbled against her skin. His hands shifted to her ass, cupping her, opening her. Her breath hitched as his fingers slid inside. In and out, he finger-fucked her. His five o'clock shadow abraded her breasts. His breath caressed her skin, his deep voice a mixture of compliments and curses, all demanding she come. *Now.*

So she did. Louder, longer and rougher than she ever had, before disintegrating on Travis's hard, muscled chest.

"Bingo."

Laughter jostled her happily sated body. "Not yet, sweetheart." He kissed her forehead and slipped out from beneath her, grinning ear-to-ear when she grumbled in protest.

Oh, the view as he walked to the dresser. Tattoos crossed his upper back, barely a break to be seen between his shoulders and the dark, thick ink work. Vines, creatures, wings? Hard to tell without a close-up investigation, but stunning nonetheless. So were his wide lats. And his ass. Especially after he shoved the boxer briefs down. Holy mother. Buns like that should be on display for women everywhere to admire. How was it even fair for a guy to have such a perfect behind?

Travis looked over his shoulder while tearing into the cardboard box. "What's with the sigh—you're not getting sleepy over there, are you?"

"Like you said before, I'm just appreciating the v—" She choked on her tongue as he turned. It'd felt big in her hand, but looking directly at it... Dear god, he intended to fuck her with that thing? "Wow, that's...impressive."

"Not really, you grabbed a box of the padded condoms."

She laughed, but still tried to scurry up to the headboard when he crawled onto the bed. "There's no such thing, I ought to know. We sell a ton of condoms in the store, and I'd sell five times as many if there was a padded variety, believe me." She wiggled her feet in mock-kicking as the beast—and his beast—stalked toward her.

His hand closed around one ankle, then the other, and

dragged her closer. Her knees brushed his sides. His palms skimmed her legs, belly, upward, to her breasts—that small stretch bringing the tip of his sheathed cock to her entrance. Every cell in her body vibrated. Every nerve ending hummed in anticipation—and a small measure of fear.

"I-I'm not sure you'll, you know... fit."

"Sweetheart, I'm flattered, but I'm not that big. Average. Maybe a bit above."

"Uh, think again. You put even my biggest dildo to shame." Blood rushed to her cheeks. "In my inventory, I mean. The store's inventory, not mine personally." Oh shit, this was getting worse with every word.

"You're so damn cute."

"Just what I wanted to hear while I'm naked in front of you."

"Nothing wrong with cute. Cute works for you."

"I'd rather be sexy. Why can't sexy work for me?" Like it did for her sister. Or the majority of women who shopped in her store.

Travis lowered his body until it subtly touched hers in every possible place. His lips moved against her skin as he spoke, starting below her ear and moving slowly downward. "It does. Your cuteness is part of what makes you sexy. Your sense of humor too—very sexy. And when I saw you for the first time, all buttoned up like a school teacher on top, but with these incredible legs that belong on a dancer... I had to stand by your counter so you wouldn't see just how sexy I found you." He punctuated the last statement with a kiss high on her inner thigh.

"Okay, I believe you," she said while sucking in a breath.

Limited was too generous a description for her experience in the oral sex department. None of what she'd received had been memorable. Sloppy and fast, zero finesse. Travis's mouth was still inches away and she was already halfway to coming.

"I don't think you do." His tongue traced the length of her slit. "I think I need to prove it to you." He added light pressure at the top, enough to bring her hips off the bed. He slid his tongue back down again, dipping inside for a little extra torture. "You're a very sexy woman, Calli. I'm going crazy from wanting you."

His warm breath tickled her sensitive skin. Beyond the words, his desire was there, woven into her name as it rolled off his talented tongue in a voice now tinged with a raspy edge.

She did believe him. She wanted him to know that.

"Travis..." She opened her eyes to find his waiting, locked on her face while he continued his sensual ministrations below her mound. Oh dear god, those eyes. The bob of his head as he continued his magic. "You make me feel sexy."

Crinkles set in at the corners of his eyes and he hummed against her clit, making her moan.

He curled his fingers into the flesh of her hips, holding her where he wanted her—tight to his mouth. The slow teasing ended as he drove his tongue at her sweet spot. Her thighs shook. Her nipples tightened and heat spread through her belly, becoming a white-hot fuse to her clit. She dug her heels into the bed, grabbed Travis's head and let go.

"Say it again," he said as he climbed over her, one knee draped over the crook of his arm.

"You make me feel sexy."

"I'm glad, but I meant my name. Say my name."

"Travis." His mouth crashed against hers. She tasted herself on his tongue, his lips, only it was different from the times she masturbated. Spicier, more intense. Because of him and the mind-blowing climaxes he'd coaxed from her body. The taste—*her taste*—sent a fresh ripple of arousal through her. She wrapped her arms around his neck, pulling him lower, forcing him to kiss her harder.

His back was firm and taut. She flattened her palms, exploring the muscles, the bumps of his spine, the divot at the base. Closer, she needed him closer.

"Travis...fuck me," she said between clashes of teeth and lips and tongues.

He groaned into her mouth. Thrust into her body. God, he was huge.

"You okay?" He'd stilled at her sucked-in breath, only partway buried. Under her palms, his ass clenched and shook—evidence of the effort it took to hold back.

"I'm good. Perfect. Don't stop."

He slid deeper. Slowly, rolling his hips, retreating and advancing. "You feel so good. So fucking good."

"So do you." The way he filled her, so completely. Each stroke brought his cock deeper inside her body, and right or wrong, closer to her heart. This was fucking, pure and glorious. But more, at least to her.

Travis caught her arms and brought them above her head. He pinned them with one hand while kissing her. Softly, erotically. Making love to her mouth while he moved inside her, over and over, bumping her clit with each pass.

"I want you to come." He breathed the words across her lips. "I want to feel you squeeze my cock while you come this time."

"I-I don't know how." The words were so pathetic. And true. Worse—the choked-up sound in her throat.

"I'll help you." He guided one of *her* hands between their bodies, chuckling when her eyes popped wide open. "You touch yourself, right, sweetheart? I know you do— you were doing it while we were online earlier."

"Yes, but—"

"No buts. That's for another time." Another wicked smile as he coaxed her hand to make circles over her clit. "Show me how you touch yourself, how you make yourself come."

Could she? Her body said yes. Travis's fingers twined with hers, following her lead. She tightened the circle. Increased the pressure and speed. The familiar thrum built inside her. Travis thrust inside her, matching her pace. She rubbed harder, faster. His hand stayed with hers, the press of his fingers adding to the frenzied climb, as if she were on an orgasm-coaster, clicking toward the summit.

And the thrilling descent.

"Oh, oh god..." She clung to him as her climax took over. Clawed at him with her left hand, pulling him deeper. Having a man inside her, filling every inch as her muscles contracted in pleasure was—

"Fuck, Calli, you're so fucking sexy, goddamn it, I have to come..." He groaned and thrust into her one more time, pushing both their bodies closer to the headboard.

She wrapped her legs around him. His cock pulsed inside her. Heavy breathing filled her head as he collapsed with his mouth near her ear, the tickle of his lips lightly brushing her skin making her shiver.

"Cold?"

"Perfectly the opposite." She extricated her hand from between them. Wet from their skin, from the heat they'd created. She threaded both hands through his thick, damp hair. "I never thought sweat could be sexy."

He shifted to his elbows, cupping her jaw and brushing his thumbs over her face. "I never thought going on that cheesy website would lead me to somebody like you."

"Like me?"

"Beautiful, hot, intriguing as hell." His lips skimmed hers for a sensual kiss. "Real. In every way."

Real. If Travis knew how boringly *real* she was, he'd hightail it out of her apartment and never play with her again—Scrabble or otherwise. He was probably used to women who went clubbing every weekend, spontaneous females who'd drop everything and come running if he called. That would never be her. They'd never be able to date. Even if she wanted to do the groupie thing, it'd be impossible. How intriguing would he find her once she told him that her life outside this building ended at sundown?

A high-pitched wail replaced the silent pause. Simultaneously, they glanced at the door, then back at each other. One look at Travis's smile and she pushed her gloomy woes to the back. Her pity party would keep for later. For now she was still the fun girl he thought he'd met online.

"I think your dog's really hating me now."

"Oh well. I happen to be really liking you."

"Let me get rid of some baggage," he slid from her body while holding the ring of the condom at the base of his cock, "and I'll get back to really liking you too."

She rolled to her side, enjoying the view as he searched her small room for the trash can. Such a fantastic body, those broad shoulders, strong legs, sexy tats. And when he ditched the condom and made the return trip to the bed—hold the phones, he was semi-hard. Again. Already.

"How can you be—" She tried to keep her eyes north of the border, but geez, how could she? "Don't you... I thought guys needed a few hours to recharge or refill their supply or something."

"You've been sadly misinformed, Ms. Yates." On his knees on the mattress, he crept alongside her, his hand slowly perusing the curves of her leg, hip, waist. "Shouldn't the owner of a sex shop know everything there is to know about sex?"

"It's a *romance* store, Travis."

A half groan, half laugh slipped out. How could she be so

cute and so hot at the same time? "You have no idea what it does to me, hearing you say my name." He slid his hand down to the curve under her ass, dragging her close enough for her to feel the effect. "Or maybe you do."

In the low light of her bedroom, her eyes were pure gray. They widened with the press of his cock against her smooth, flat belly. Gorgeous. He skimmed up her back to her hair. Sifting through it like a kid at the beach. Only it was silkier than any sand he'd ever touched. He brought a handful of it over her shoulder. Buried his nose in it and inhaled. Roses. Sweet as summertime. He closed his eyes and breathed it in again, then moved to her neck. He could damn well eat her up, she smelled so good.

"What are you doing?" The question came on a gasp as he worked his way down her body with stops at each nipple, her navel, then the top of her sweet, sweet pussy.

"Having more of you."

She let him roll her onto her back and settle between her thighs. The cooperation ended there, her delicate hand with its long, purple nails cupping her sex.

Denied access to his target, he dragged his tongue along the crevice between her fingers. Showing her what he wanted to do—intended to do—when she gave up her game of hide and seek.

Her eyes were dark, the irises almost nonexistent. Her tits rose and fell quickly. She even whimpered a little when he swirled his tongue over the apex of her index and middle fingers, directly above her clit. Shouldn't be much longer now.

"Shouldn't I go freshen up before you," she bit into her lip, "you know, do that... again?"

Not a game, then. True innocence. Or insecurity. Whatever it was, it stirred something inside him. Some primal need to protect and reassure, to open her up, make her release and revel in her sexuality, then to keep her all to himself. His cock jerked beneath him and it was all he could do not to rip her hand away and take her with his mouth and fingers, then slide his cock deep into her body and claim full ownership. She brought out some dormant caveman gene he'd never experienced before—and it was one hell of an aphrodisiac.

But those eyes, staring down at him, so apprehensively, forced him to rein the caveman in. For now.

"I'm here because I want to be, because you smell incredible and taste so sweet. Because making you come—watching you give yourself over to me—is the sexiest thing I've ever seen. Let me in, sweetheart."

Her grip loosened.

Gently, he peeled her fingers back and moved her hand aside. The heat and scent of her arousal washed over him, followed by a ripple of gut-deep need. The caveman surged to the surface. "Tell me I can have you—that every inch of you is mine."

"Have me. I-I'm yours."

The words, her voice, those eyes staring into his—undid him. There'd be no slow and easy this time. He wasn't stopping until Calli screamed his name. He covered her with his mouth, penetrating her with his tongue. Still so wet—for him. And delicious, even better than the first time. He drew her clit between his lips to suckle it. Her hips bucked upward, her fingers curling into his hair. Riding his face from the bottom—holy fuck.

Her eyes were closed. Tits heaving. Mouth open as she panted and moaned. Hot, damn hot, but not enough. He wanted her desperate. Wanted her to fly off the edge for the sheer pleasure of the fall.

With his left hand, he reached up and rolled her nipple between his fingers. She arched into the touch. He squeezed, she gasped. He plucked harder, she moaned. Fuck.

He stroked her slit. His cock ached, it wanted in her so badly. He thrust his hips against the bed. Slid two fingers inside her pussy. She clenched around them instantly, hugging him. Jesus, it was going to feel so good when he fucked her. He curled his fingers toward her belly, scissoring them, dragging his fingertips across her G-spot. She cried out, her whole body shaking with the onset of climax. Still wasn't enough. He slanted his hand. Tickled the ring of her ass with his pinky using small brushes across and around. Then he pushed inside—tip only, wiggling it until she relaxed, then deeper, deeper, until he was surrounded by tight heat to the second knuckle—and her voice, filling the air and his head.

"Travis, oh god, Travis..."

Again and again, she cried his name. Whimpering, moaning, begging. For all the music he'd heard in his lifetime, nothing had ever been more satisfying to his ears.

As hard as she'd clawed at him, holding him tight to her throbbing sex seconds earlier, she now pushed him away.

"Stop, stop, get up here and fuck me." She looked straight into his soul while licking those luscious lips. "Have me—every inch of me."

"Every inch?" The beast inside him roared. "Careful what you offer, sweetheart."

Her eyes flickered. And then she rolled, giving him a primo view of the sweetest ass he'd ever seen. "Every inch... all yours... *Travis.*"

He couldn't get to the damn dresser fast enough, tripping off the bed in the process. Behind him, she giggled at his stumbling and fumbling with the condom box. An innocent sound, it still made his cock jerk against his stomach.

He ripped open the foil, started to smooth on the condom. Then he heard it—an intermittent whining in a disturbingly low tone. The dog. He glanced at the door, then to the bed. Calli, waving her finery at him. The most beautiful come-fuck-me eyes blinking at him while she bit into her lower lip. She hadn't heard the noise on the other side of the door, obviously.

Damn. Damn, damn. The rescuer in him pushed every other version of himself to the background. He tossed the condom on the dresser and went to the door, covering his goods with one hand while he cracked the painted wood a few inches.

"Travis?"

"I heard something. Your dog was whining. Stay put, I'm checking it out." One look at the Chihuahua and their night was done. At least the pleasure parts. "Oh fuck."

"What? What's wrong?"

In his peripheral vision, he saw her bounce off the bed and come up behind him. He closed the door to shield her view. "He's hurt. In pain, but not bleeding." At least, not that he'd seen in his quick perusal.

"Oh my god, no. Let me out, let me see him." For a little woman, she had strength enough to wrench the doorknob away and push past him. She dropped to her knees in the hallway, hands moving everywhere but touching nothing. "Charming, shh, it's okay, it's okay." She looked up at Travis, eyes full of fear. "What could've happened to him?"

"Looks like he's dislocated his leg from the shoulder socket maybe." If not broken it, but he wasn't about to offer that up. "We need to get him to an emergency clinic. Where's the closest one?"

The fear he'd seen in her eyes turned to panic. "I don't know. And I can't take him. I can't go out in—this."

"Because of the snowstorm? I'll drive. You can sit in the back with him, keep him still as possible."

Tears welled in her eyes, dropping like big, fat raindrops onto her cheeks. Her shoulders slumped and she dropped her head, blanketing her little dog with her long, dark hair. "I can't. You don't understand—I just can't."

Damn right he didn't understand. "What do you mean, you can't? He's going to be in agony until a vet deals with his leg."

This wasn't something to debate—the dog needed professional help, now. Period. Each second she sat there sobbing and silent, his confusion bubbled closer to anger. And it wasn't even his fucking dog. He collected his clothes from the bedroom and living room. Threw them on and returned to the hall. The dog hadn't stopped whining and was shaking all over, yet she hadn't budged. What the hell?

"Calli. We need to go." Still no movement. *"Calli."*

"I can't," she whispered, finally lifting her face. "I don't go out when it's dark."

He laughed out loud. How could he not—her statement was so screwed-up it was funny. "Your dog is suffering but you won't take him to the vet because you're scared of the dark?"

"Not won't, *can't.* I've tried, I try every night. I freeze up—it's…impossible."

Oh shit, more tears. He braced for the flight response the sight of female tears always initiated.

"I know how pathetic I am." She tugged her knees up to her chest. "I could use some help."

"Yeah, I guess so." He silently cursed for letting the asswipe side of himself get access to his mouth. "I'm sorry—I didn't mean—"

"It's okay." She swiped at her face, then pushed to her feet and brushed past him into the bedroom where she dressed in jeans and a sweatshirt as fast as humanly possible. "You should leave. I have to call my sister to come over and I don't feel like answering questions about you tonight."

There it was. His free ticket to get-the-fuck-out-of-there land. But his feet didn't take a single step.

She stared him down. "I'm sorry you didn't get to-to—finish everything we were doing. You can come back and collect some other time if you want—I'll give you what you were expecting."

"Jesus, is that what you think's going through my

head? That I'm not leaving until I fuck you again?"

"Isn't it?" She looked away, tapping on the numeric pad of the portable in her hand.

"Put the phone down."

She didn't comply, just met his stare with cold eyes. Why weren't his feet heading down the stairs and out the door?

"Hey," Calli said into the receiver. "Charming is hurt, can you take—"

He snatched the phone from her hand. "She doesn't need you. Have a good night."

It rang almost immediately. Calli grabbed for it— denied. He wasn't the tallest guy in the world, but he had enough on her to keep it out of reach.

"Give me the phone." Her jump and swipe at his arm almost made him laugh. "If I don't answer, she'll freak out—I never have men here."

"So you said." He pressed the end button, only to have the ringing resume twenty seconds later.

"She'll call the police."

"Fine." He punched the talk key and cupped the phone to his head. "Caitlyn, I'm a friend of your sister's. Her dog has a badly injured leg, probably from throwing himself at the bedroom door while I was making Calli scream during her orgasm. I'm heading to the vet's now. Calli will call you later with an update." He thrust the phone at Calli, whose mouth was hanging about to her knees. "Get me an address and some blankets to wrap," he gritted his teeth, "*Prince Charming* with."

The drive to the after-hours animal clinic had been slow and tense. Terrified, pain-stricken dog in the backseat of his Nissan. White-out conditions on the roads. And a thousand questions about Calli swirling in his brain.

Why was she afraid of the dark? Since when? What did she do every night, confined to a tiny apartment? Is that why she hadn't been with a man in so long, or was there some other reason? Where the hell were her family and friends... why weren't they doing something to help her with her phobia? And the million-dollar question—was *he* going to try?

Travis leaned back in the uncomfortable vinyl waiting-room chairs. Somewhere beyond the *Clinic Staff Only* door, Calli's Chihuahua was probably scared shitless. He'd tried to go back with the dog, but the nurse—technician, assistant, whatever the proper term for them was—had waved him off. Not a sight for the faint of heart, she'd told him. Did he look the type to pass out during a veterinary exam? Probably, if she thought a pocket-sized canine named Charming was his. Safe to say she thought he was off the market to women too.

What did he care, anyway? Not his dog. Not his girlfriend's dog. Hell, not even his friend's dog, though he'd called himself that on the phone to Calli's sister. But he wanted to be. Friends at minimum, more since their evening together.

He closed his eyes, replaying the best parts of tonight. Calli's eyes were up there on the list. Her hair. And lips. Hell, everything about her face was gorgeous. Body too. She had these incredible curves—full tits, a handful of a waist, insanely perfect ass. And between her legs... pure heaven.

Every second of the sex had been real, connected. Completely lacking the porno phoniness that had become his dating life since Black Box accumulated a following.

He liked Calli's mind too. Sense of humor, quick with a witty comeback. She made him smile. And a single woman who owned and ran her own business—that was impressive. It took initiative, guts and perseverance. It took spunk and control. So what was her crazy deal with the fear of darkness?

The Calli in the sobbing heap at his feet, calling herself pathetic, paralyzed at the idea of setting foot outside at nighttime...that wasn't the same girl he'd met online, played dirty Scrabble against or gotten hard and sweaty with. She might be more than a little bit nuts. Probably somebody he should chalk up as an amazing one-night stand and leave it at that. Drop off her mended dog and drive off into the snowsquall.

His cell buzzed with a text notification. Had to be Calli, checking in. He yanked it from his pocket so fast it clattered to the linoleum, the noise and his accompanying curse echoing off the sterile white walls. Oh yeah, that plan to wave and walk away should work out really well.

It's Calli. Sorry to bother you. Any word yet?

Nothing since they took him to an exam room. They wouldn't let me go with him.

You tried? That was nice of you. Thank you. For that, and the rest of it too.

The rest of it. She probably meant bringing her dog across the tri-cities at 10:30 p.m. in a blizzard. But he couldn't leave it at a simple statement of polite conversation.

Making you come was entirely my pleasure, no thanks required.

A wall clock ticked off a long, loud minute before his cell vibrated with her reply.

Tonight was the best night of my life. Another message popped up seconds later. *I bet you get that a lot.*

Yeah, he'd heard it before. This time it didn't make his eyes roll—it made his mouth stretch into a big old grin. Before he could tap in a message, a white-coated woman with a stethoscope around her neck pushed through the door.

"Mr. Graham? You can see your dog now."

Vet just called me in to see your dog. Text you soon. He slid the phone into his pocket and followed the woman. What was it with medical places—always white or gray, never real colors that'd put the unlucky visitors at ease.

They passed several doors before Dr. Millen, as she'd introduced herself, motioned him into a large room with metal cages on two walls. Holding cells. Charming was in an upper unit, purple Kling wrap covering a section of the right front leg.

"He's standing." Travis stepped closer to the cage for a better look. "Should he be standing?"

The doc curled her hand around his forearm—a friendlier gesture than necessary, one that went with her eyes as she looked *him* over, head to toe, finishing with a sweep of tongue across what looked suspiciously like freshly glossed lips. "It's sweet to see a man so attached to his pet."

"He's my girlfriend's dog." The statement rolled from out of his mouth automatically. No hesitation, even with the very attractive vet practically offering herself up on a stainless-steel surgical table.

"Oh, well then." She stuffed her hands into her lab coat pockets and focused on the patient. "Simple acquired luxation resulting from trauma, not an underlying condition. Radiographs showed no breaks or fractures. We gave him a mild sedative for relaxation and performed a manual relocation. The tape is merely to beef up support—it can come off tomorrow. No running, jumping or exertion for a week. I'll go enter his case details in the computer. You can pick up his anti-inflammatories at the desk where you pay."

Calli had shoved a wad of cash in his hand before he left her place. After settling Charming's tab—probably padded by the disgruntled lady vet—she wouldn't be getting much change. Running a business, she'd have to be smart with her money. This little excursion had cost over four hundred dollars. Even if the cash had come from rainy-day savings, the total was a stinger.

He bet Calli wouldn't blink—that she'd only care her dog was home in one piece. He had no basis for the feeling, just a nagging in his gut that demanded he keep her around, invest some time getting to know her better. And his gut was a hell of a lot more fickle than his dick. Since both parts had a thing for Calli, he was inclined to listen.

He parked in front of her building and pulled out his cell. *We're back. Be at your door in two minutes.*

"Come on, tough guy," he said, scooping the dog from

the shotgun seat to his lap. The car had been off less than a minute and a film of ice covered the windshield. The Chihuahua was already shaking and Travis hadn't opened the door yet. "Shit." He'd forgotten the damn blanket at the emergency clinic. "Guess it's inside the coat for you."

He pulled his hat down over his ears and tucked his scarf around the tiny head poking out of his lapels, then hustled around back.

Calli was peeking through the blinds when he reached the door. Metal clicked and scraped as she unlocked her system of deadbolts and slides. She'd known he was mere yards away, yet she hadn't opened the door in advance. Whatever her issue was, it had a seriously firm hold over her.

He didn't need a woman with baggage. Didn't have time for a relationship that had *project* written all over it. Yet when she opened the door with a huge, genuine smile on her face, he knew he'd just signed on for the job.

Chapter Seven

Calli had hauled a folded metal dog crate up the stairs herself, refusing his offer of help. She'd all but ignored him as she took her dog into the bedroom to settle him. A good ten minutes later, she exited the bedroom, coming to an abrupt stop when she saw him leaning on the back of her couch.

"I thought you would've left."

"You didn't tell me I had to."

The wheels turned behind her pretty eyes. "I'm glad you're still here, actually."

"Good. Me too."

She pulled some folded bills from her back pocket, stepped closer and extended her hand. "Take it. As a thank you for your trouble. And for the gas you used."

He crossed his arms over his chest. "I didn't hang around so you'd give me money."

"Oh..." Several silent minutes ticked away as the tension between them thickened uncomfortably. "I forgot what I promised you earlier." She met his eyes for a second. Bit her lip and sighed. Tucked the cash away then went to work on the button and zipper of her jeans.

He pushed off the couch to a stand before she had the jeans shimmied past the curve of her hip. "Not that I'm in any way opposed to seeing you naked again, but what are you doing?"

"You didn't leave and you don't want money, so I figured you wanted to finish up... from before."

"And that's okay with you."

She didn't answer. Not with words. The way her hand fiddled with the zipper instead of getting on with the strip show told the truth. The jeans stayed put. Low enough to give him a view of the smooth skin below her stomach. High enough to tease the crap out of him without even trying.

"I'm not fucking you to balance some invisible ledger." Much to the chagrin of his aching cock.

"Is it the weather—are the roads too bad? You can sleep over," a burn of red flooded her cheeks, "on the couch, I mean. I'll get some blankets and a—"

He cuffed her wrist before she could escape to the linen closet. "The driving is no big deal."

She let out a long sigh. "I'm not altogether lacking in the intelligence department, Travis, but I don't get why you're still here."

Any last-minute reservations he had melted into the background when she called him by name. "I'd like to finish our Scrabble game."

"But you just said you didn't want to," she looked up at him with eyes that matched her exasperated voice, "you know... fuck me."

"I never said I didn't want to. Only that I wouldn't do it as part of some payment plan." He tugged her closer and she didn't resist, letting him pull her tight against his chest and the hard bulge in his pants. But it wasn't just about that, for once in his life. "I was a jerk earlier. I regret that." Not the greatest apology. Didn't matter what her issue with the darkness was, she hadn't deserved the treatment he'd dished out. He hated that he'd hurt her, that his shitty former self had made an appearance, even for a second.

From the way she melted, sliding her arms around his waist, she accepted his half-assed apology for what it was. Forgave his stupid ass. He'd take it, and this time, he wouldn't screw it up.

"Two in the morning is kind of late for Scrabble, plus I already put the board away." Good night and goodbye words, yet she didn't move. Just stared up at him with big, beautiful, unsure eyes. "Do you want to stay and...?" She flicked a glance at the bedroom.

"Be with you. Talk. Get to know each other better."

A furrow set up residence between her eyebrows. Damn, it made her even cuter. More irresistible.

"You really don't want to know more about me. I'm a train wreck, if you hadn't figured that out for yourself."

"Yeah, but you're a hot, cute, funny and smart train wreck. Let's compare baggage and see who's more screwed-up."

She snickered and shook her head. "You're going to lose this one."

He slid his hands lower, over the strip of exposed skin

at the top of her shoved-down jeans. "I doubt that, sweetheart."

The clock on the television said they'd been talking over an hour. Side by side at first, until he'd stretched his arm over the back of the couch and pulled her closer, into a cuddle. They'd started with small stuff, likes and dislikes— food, movies, music, etcetera. Verbal personal résumés, essentially.

Then Travis had freely offered up his baggage. A history of bouncing, and not the enforcer-at-a-bar kind. He'd started three post-secondary programs and finished none. Statistics at university for a year. Two years of college learning the ins-and-outs of code and computer programming. Two years apprenticing with an electrician. Assorted odd jobs in between. Not that he was a slacker, he'd always found solid means to pay the bills—the current method being freelance website design—but the only thing that'd truly stuck in his life was music.

His personal track record was equally bumpy. He'd moved around—six cities and twice as many apartments since leaving his parents' home at eighteen. Tight with his family, but no serious romantic relationships, ever. Just a very lengthy string of casual encounters and broken hearts, though he denied that last part.

Not the kind of guy she should be getting involved with, but here she was, in his arms, having the best night of her life. Forcing her eyes to stay open so it wouldn't end. Being with Travis was easy. Automatic, like blinking. It didn't make sense, but she liked it.

She yawned, not subtly enough to sneak it past him.

"Here, let's do this." He shifted to a lying position while cupping her leg and draping her half on top of him. "Good?"

"Mmm-hmm."

Cradling her with one arm, he reached across their bodies to stroke her hair with the other. "You have incredible hair." He threaded his fingertips through its length, crown to ends, then back to the top to make the journey, over and over.

Safety, comfort, sensuality. She wrapped her arm around his waist, snuggled into the spot where his chest joined his shoulder. Bliss, pure and simple.

"Do you ever leave the building?"

So much for bliss. And simple. "In the daytime, yes."

"Never at night?"

"Not for the past two years, no."

"Tell me about it."

She hadn't talked about the attack since quitting therapy eighteen months ago. The majority of inquiries from family and acquaintances had stopped around the one-year mark. There'd been nobody new in her life to tell—until now. For him, a chance at whatever this connection was between them, she'd relive that night.

"It happened December 22, three weeks after I opened Romance U. The bank is only a few blocks away. I figured I'd drop off the day's deposit and grab a pita to go on the way back, like I'd done most nights. A man walked by, your average guy, nothing about him stood out or set off any alarms for me. I even smiled at him—I was on top of the world, so why not, right? Then I looked down to dig the deposit bag from my purse and—" Now her pulse sped up. She released a long, low breath. "It happened so fast. A greasy palm slapped over my mouth. He wrenched my arms back and hauled me into an alley." Her stomach and chest clenched. One deep, heaving sob escaped.

Travis's body stiffened under hers. "You don't have to tell me the rest."

"I do, so you understand. I just need," another hiccup-like sob racked her body, "a sec to regroup."

His arms folded around her, pulling her tighter to his body. "Take it slow, I'm not going anywhere."

"He, he..." She touched her throat, she always did while remembering. "He pinned me against the wall with one hand. So hard, god it hurt." She swallowed. Tried clearing her throat, but it was too dry, too tight. "He squeezed my neck. I cried, I would've begged for mercy, but I couldn't talk. He punched me. In the temple, then in the stomach and chest. I couldn't breathe. Everything went black and I thought I was going to die. Then I heard him laughing, and the sound of cloth ripping, buttons falling to the pavement, and I wished I *would* die before he...oh god."

"Shh, sweetheart, shh..." He rocked her, pressed his lips to her head.

She barely registered the actions, Travis's voice. The gates were open and nothing would stop all of it from tumbling out on choppy breaths. "He left me there, unconscious. I didn't know if he'd—if he'd—you know." The word refused to come out. "The ER doctor had to do an internal exam."

"What did it tell them?" Travis's voice was as hoarse as hers.

She shook her head against the safe haven of his chest. "He didn't rape me."

"Thank god."

"My coat and blouse were torn, so was my skirt. The police officer said the attacker either got scared off before he could finish, or..." She gulped for air. Replaying it brought it all back, as if it'd been yesterday.

"Calli, stop."

Not now that she'd gotten this far. "Or I might've gotten lucky by passing out, because some monsters get more pleasure out of inciting fear than the sex part of...rape. That bastard broke my hyoid bone, damaged my trachea, cracked a rib, gave me a nasty black eye. I'm stuck inside indefinitely and my voice has never been the same...and I should consider myself *lucky*."

"Sick motherfucker. Did they catch him?"

"No." And that's what it boiled down to at sunset every day. That man, the vicious animal who hadn't finished with her, was still out there. Maybe living in her neighborhood. "I hate what he did to me, physically, but I got past it. I don't jump when somebody gets close to me, or brushes by me in the grocery store, like I used to. But the panic when I try setting foot out the door at night—I hate him most of all for that."

Travis said nothing. Just held her and kissed her. Stroked her hair and back while her breathing slowed to normal. Let her soak his shirt with useless tears until they'd run their course.

"I'm sorry for earlier. I couldn't have been a bigger asshole if I'd tried."

"You didn't know, but thank you."

"Hey..." Travis gently hooked her under the chin, tipping her head up to meet his eyes. Intense, but also so, so sweet. "Nobody, and I mean nobody, is going to hurt you while I'm around."

"Okay." How'd they get from anonymous online Scrabble to this? Relief settled over her. She'd told him and he hadn't run. Instead of ridicule, he'd offered to protect her. She burrowed as close as possible. Travis Graham, tattooed mega-hottie, had become her living, breathing security blanket. God help her when she'd have to let him go.

Charming's whining and scratching roused Calli from a wonderful dream. She lifted her head from the pillow— only it wasn't a pillow, it was Travis's chest. And some of the amazing dream had been real.

The living room lamp was still on, giving her a decent view of the man sharing her couch. God, he was gorgeous, even while sleeping. A dark shadow of stubble covered his jaw, highlighting the small dimple in his chin. Awake and smiling, Travis lit up her world, but seeing his mouth completely still, set in a straight line—she itched to touch it, his lips were so full and appealing. He muttered something incoherent and turned his head to one side. Disheveled hair stuck out in several directions.

She slid her hand up his chest, pausing briefly over his

sleep-slowed, steady heartbeat, and threaded her fingers into his hair. Another mumble. A little tick of a smile. His arm against her back tightened, his fingers making circles against her sweatshirt.

"Pull it up."

Her eyes snapped to his face. Not so much as a flutter to be seen across his eyelids. How long had he been awake, lying there still and silent? She shuffled, inching the fleece top upward until his fingers connected with her skin.

"Better."

Wasn't it just? His hand slid up, leaving a trail of sparks that ended at the curve of her breast, where he continued to stroke bare flesh. He adjusted his leg, inserting it squarely between her thighs, against the crotch of her jeans. The seam pressed on her clit. Well, *that* part of her body was wide awake now. She shifted slightly—and subtly, she hoped. A small move to the right and bingo— sweet spot achieved. Travis pushed his leg tighter. His fingers found her nipple. She barely had time to catch a breath before it hit—a small, intense burst of sensation radiating from her clit. He'd made her come again. Fully clothed, only partially awake, while barely moving. Good god.

This time when she looked up, his eyes were open. And his smile was lethal sexy.

"I wouldn't mind if you kept playing with that," he arched an eyebrow and nodded at her hand gripping the bulge in his jeans, "but I think your dog needs to go out."

She disentangled herself, grudgingly. Because wow, he smelled incredible. All sleepy and sexy and warm...yum. If she didn't move immediately, her little dog might damage himself again, this time while trying to escape his crate for a pee.

Travis stopped her by curling a palm around her hamstring. "It's still dark outside, let me take him."

"Don't worry, he has a litter box inside."

"Can he lift his leg in it?"

"No, he squats."

"Not while I'm here. Men weren't made to *squat* while taking a leak, sweetheart." Travis pushed up from the comfort of the couch and ran his fingers through that thick, adorably sexy bedhead while she collected Charming and his leash.

Until last night, her dad was the only man Charming had spent any time with. Yet the way her little dog settled into Travis's arms, you'd think he'd been there hundreds of times. Travis didn't appear to mind, either. This wouldn't become an everyday sight—her logical, practical side knew that. That didn't stop her heart from doing a fluttery dance. Wanting was such a dangerous thing.

She followed them down the stairs. Travis smiled as she unfastened her system of locks. Not a sympathetic now-I-understand kind of smile. Something much sweeter. Something she couldn't put a description to.

"We'll be back in a couple of minutes," he said, and she closed the door behind them.

She stood with her hands pressed to the cold glass, watching. Six thirty in the morning and Travis was walking her dog. Unbelievable. First, the volcanically hot sex. Then talking for hours. At some point, they'd fallen asleep wrapped around each other. She'd met him less than twenty-four hours ago and that just didn't seem possible.

Travis came into view and she couldn't hold back the smile. Snow dotted his hair. Clouds of fog escaped his mouth as he spoke to the little dog at his side. No sign of discomfort coming from Charming now. Travis was good medicine for her *and* her dog.

"I think you have a new fan," she said as they came through the door. "He's going to be giving me the bug-eyed death glare next time I make him use his indoor facilities."

"Don't make him. I'll come by after the store is closed. We can take him out together."

"I can't go out then. I thought you understood that now."

Travis's hands rested lightly on her shoulders, as cold from the minutes in the pre-dawn air as his eyes were warm. "I understand why you're afraid to go out alone at night, sweetheart. You won't be alone. You'll be safe with me."

"It won't work."

"You won't even try?"

"You think I haven't? With my parents, my sister... hell, Travis, even with the cop from the night of the incident. Over and over, I've tried going out *there* after dark," she stabbed a finger toward the door, "and I can't do it."

He withdrew his touch, crossing his arms high on his chest. A new chill emanated from him. This one reached his eyes. "You haven't tried with me."

"Seriously? You're going to make this about you?"

"I'm making it about us."

"Telling you about the attack doesn't mean I can suddenly decide to go out and just... go out. It's not that simple."

"So, what—you're going to stay inside for the rest of your life?"

"If I have to."

"Come on, Calli, do something about it, take control. Join a self-defense class, buy pepper spray or a gun. Hell, go for both. Get a shrink or hypnosis."

Heat built inside her chest, spreading to her face, making her temples throb. "Check to everything except the gun. Nothing works."

"That's crazy."

"Ding, ding, ding. Now you get it—and me." How dare he judge her? And how stupid of her to think he wouldn't. She scooped Charming into her arms and pulled open the door, inviting a blast of frigid November air into the entryway. "I think it'd be best if..." God, everything was changing too fast. "Thank you, for... everything."

Thank god for the boxes of stock that arrived after lunch. Unpacking, steaming and ticketing merchandise kept Calli's hands busy, even if her mind stayed on a certain Scrabble-playing, orgasm-giving man every single second.

She hadn't kicked him out this morning, not exactly,

but he hadn't put up any argument when she showed him the door. Why would he? No, Travis wasn't perfect. He'd admitted to a less-than-admirable track record with women during his party-boy days. Also to having an unhealthy amount of ego.

Those flaws didn't compare to her list of shortcomings. They'd hit it off, had some fun and a few hours of heart-deep conversation. That didn't mean they were dating. She'd never be able to *date* anybody, not truly, and certainly not a man like Travis.

Motion caught her eye, pulling her from her pity party. Caitlyn was halfway to the back of the store. Something must be out of whack with the door sensor, because this was the third time today it hadn't buzzed when opened. Great, another unexpected expense.

"What's up with all the sighing?" Caitlyn picked up one of the packages Calli was shelving in Romance U's *Spicy Nights* corner. "Ooh, now I understand. Mr. Right Magnum Eight. Yup, he does kinda make a girl want to sigh." She scanned the product features and snorted. "Whisper-quiet. They all say that. How was it when you tried it out?"

"What do you think I did, Cait? Flipped the sign on the door, slapped the *mighty-hold suction cup* on my desk in the back room and went for a joy ride? I haven't tried it." She left off the *yet*. But she totally had one set aside for later. Mr. Right was no Travis Graham, but that stud had galloped away.

Caitlyn's robust laugh filled the store. "I meant, have you put batteries in one and compared the noise level to other models—in a dry run—like you always do."

"Oh. Well, no."

"Hmm. My sister off her game…interesting."

With the few details Caitlyn knew about last night, she wasn't likely to let this opportunity pass. Caitlyn didn't talk while they powered up an ivory Mr. Right Magnum Eight and tested his variable settings and functions, but the smug smile never left her face. Saving her best remarks until they'd completed their examination of the whopper dildo, no doubt.

"He's not so quiet, this Mr. Right." Caitlyn ran a hand up and down his length. "And he's extremely hard. Like, maybe too rigid for some stuff. What d'ya think?"

"Ugh, I hope not. I got two cases of twelve—I'd hate to send them back so close to Christmas. Let me see." Calli swapped spots so she could get a better grip on Mr. Right where they'd attached him to the glass-top case. He was definitely a handful—one point in his favor. "Hmm. You're right about him being overly rigid. But the veins are nice and the cock head is probably the most impressive one I've seen." She stroked upward again, the PVC shaft creating more drag against her palm than she'd like. "He'd certainly require lube, especially for anal use."

Caitlyn was grinning at her like a schoolgirl caught with a *Playgirl* magazine.

"What?" Calli asked. "You know people will want to use him that way. His suction cup and scrotum make him perfect for anal—no worries about him getting lost up there in the heat of the moment."

Caitlyn licked her lips as she straightened, her focus no longer on the sex toy's attributes.

Calli turned her head, following Caitlyn's sightline. Oh, shit. Shit, shit, shit.

"Don't stop *working* on my account, ladies." Travis weaved around racks of lingerie that got racier the farther into the store he walked.

Caught with one hand wrapped around a big, plastic cock and the second one cupping its balls. And the stuff she'd said... Calli's face burned with the heat of a struck match. After the way things had ended at the bottom of her apartment stairs, she hadn't expected to see Travis again. Certainly not so soon, or sporting a smile that made her glad for the absorbent cotton gusset in her bikini panties. She kept her head down, fumbling to get Mr. Right Magnum Eight back into his package before Travis reached the back of the store.

"Cal, you forgot to take out the batteries. Saving that one for later?"

Oh, nice. Caitlyn couldn't have said that any louder or clearer, could she?

Calli shot her sister the death look. She stretched over the counter, scrambling to shove the enormous plastic package amongst the dark shopping bags they used to ensure discretion. But Mr. Right refused to be crammed into a small space—no surprise there. The package dropped to the floor, where Mr. Right burst out of his plastic housing and began vibrating in earnest against the polished-concrete floor. Kind of gave new meaning to the term *dry humping*.

"That's something you don't see every day," Travis said. The grin on his face grew while she scurried around the counter to trap and contain the rogue vibrating mega-dildo.

Calli peeked up through the screen of her eyelashes. Despite Caitlyn having repositioned her gorgeous, outgoing self at Travis's elbow with her high-sheen lips pulled into her patented sexy pout, he didn't give her a second look. Catching Calli's glance, he winked.

She flushed hotter and dropped her eyes to the task at hand. Without seeing, though, she knew exactly where Travis was looking—the heated trail down her spine, over her ass and along her legs gave it away. A wave of dizziness washed over her, despite being on all fours. Or maybe that was part of the reason. That's how she'd been before the action had screeched to a halt last night—in the doggie position, waving her booty at him and ready for something much more fun than the toy now safely back in its box.

"I'm glad you decided to come back," Caitlyn said, moving her hand into direct contact with Travis's, on the frosted glass countertop.

Calli brushed invisible dust from her hands and knees, standing back while Caitlyn did her flirt thing, oblivious to the attention she *wasn't* getting from Travis. Calli snorted. Actually snorted at her sister—smirked too, the corners of her lips drawing upward despite her best attempts to keep them down. Not that it mattered. Caitlyn was so absorbed in Travis, she didn't register either action. When it came to men, there'd never been any competition between them. Caitlyn got the hot, popular guys, Calli didn't.

Until this one.

Travis looked from Calli to Caitlyn, then back. "I had to come back…my wallet must've fallen out of my jeans in Calli's apartment last night." He flicked a quick glance at Caitlyn's dropped jaw, then gifted Calli with a naughty smile. "Probably when you were picking your panties out of my back pocket."

"Oh my god. Oh. My. God. *This* is the guy you slept with last night?"

In her entire life, Calli'd never seen her sister in this state. Completely lacking in cool self-confidence. Flabbergasted. Karma might get her for this, but what the hell—Calli kept her chin up and savored the moment.

"How?" Caitlyn's question bordered on sputtering.

"I met Calli playing online Scrabble. I couldn't stop thinking about her, so I pieced together her clues and found her. Sort of." He glanced at Caitlyn. "That mix-up between us the other day—entirely my fault, sorry."

"You came in here looking for her, not me," Caitlyn said.

Yes, it was a first, but did Caitlyn have to drip disbelief all over the floor? Geez.

"I should've been more straightforward, but I didn't want to freak Calli—who I thought you were—out."

"Yeah, I suppose not, since you essentially cyber-stalked her whereabouts."

"*Cait.*"

"Well, didn't he?"

"No—I told him parts of my name, the city and the slogan of the store. I think I—" In retrospect, she'd been far from anonymous. "Part of me wanted him to find me." She met Travis's gaze and held it. "I hoped he would."

"Did you know who *he* was?"

Warmth spread through Calli's veins. "No, not really.

Just some word nerd with a flower for a picture and a dirty sense of humor who claimed to play guitar."

"Wow." Caitlyn pinched the bridge of her nose between two hot-pink-lacquered fingers. She shook her head, then stared at Calli again. "You, of all people, led a complete stranger to your door. Do you know how dangerous that was?"

This from the woman who'd been encouraging her to join Plenty of Fish or Match.com. Something smelled rotten and looked green. Caitlyn, jealous of *her*. Much as she wanted to call Caitlyn on it, the words didn't come.

"Can you watch the store for a couple of minutes while I find Travis's wallet?"

"I'll help you look," he said, less than two steps behind her.

Caitlyn released an exaggerated sigh and shrugged out of her jacket. "I have places to be, Cal... save your *Scrabble playing* for afterhours."

Travis followed her through her office-slash-stockroom to the door leading to her apartment stairs. He didn't touch her, didn't need to. Her skin remembered the sensation of his fingers, palms, tongue, exploring every inch of its surface, every curve and divot. With each stair she climbed, her breasts shifted inside the black demi-bra. The lace scraped her nipples. They tightened, pulling some invisible string running directly between her legs, making her clit ache for contact.

The incidental brush of Travis's arm across her hip as he palmed the railing fanned the flame to a roaring blaze. Above the tops of her stockings, her thighs went from moist to slick. She tried squeezing them together as she stepped. The clenching merely added to the friction, making it worse. Much worse. Oh god, if she could smell it—the telltale scent of horny woman—he had to be able to. Especially being two risers below her.

"If you'd called or messaged me, I could've looked for your wallet earlier and had it waiting." Downstairs, in a public setting. Safer—sexually speaking.

Inside the apartment, she made a beeline for the couch while Charming went bananas over Travis. Yeah, she knew how the little dog felt, unfortunately.

"He looks pretty spry. You took the wrap off his leg."

"No," she said while digging between the couch cushions. "*He* took it off. While I was in the shower, the naughty little bugger."

Travis laughed. "I don't blame him. I prefer to be naked around you too."

Her head snapped up to find him in a crouch. Petting the dog, but unabashedly staring at her ass and legs. And why not—she'd practically given him an engraved invitation, bending over the sofa in a short skirt and calf-high black boots. Instinctively, she smoothed the black twill with one hand, over the curve of her butt to the bottom of the skirt. Her fingers met a thin strip of bare skin instead of nylon stockings. She coasted along the exposed, hot flesh until she encountered the strap of her garter.

"Do you always dress this way?"

"Skirts instead of pants?" The wallet was in her right hand, still buried between the cushions. She didn't move from her compromising position. Couldn't. Not with

Travis's gaze glued to her body, his tongue swiping across those Greek-god lips.

"In sexy lingerie," he said, standing and taking a step toward her.

"No, not always." Oh god, he was right behind her. His jeans brushed her hamstrings. Such a fleeting touch. Not enough, not nearly enough.

"I didn't mean to upset you this morning… that was the jerk version of me I told you about last night. I wish he hadn't come out with you."

She straightened and faced him, wallet in hand. "And I wish I wasn't the irrational, neurotic woman I told you about last night, but I am."

One of them should say something else. Travis took the wallet, tucked it in his back pocket. She transferred her weight foot to foot and back again. They looked at one another but said nothing. A standoff—until Charming barked up at them. The moment had a distinctly domestic feeling, as if the little dog was telling them to kiss, make up and move on. Would that it was so simple.

"I should take him out for a minute and get back to the store before Caitlyn has a shit fit."

"I'll follow you out, I've got to get some test pages to a client before he joins your sister in shit fit land. Once people decide they're ready for a new website, they want it done yesterday."

Normal conversation. This, she could do. "So, if I told you I want my online store redesigned, when could I expect to have it done? Yesterday?"

She gasped as he cupped her waist, dragging her tight

and close to his body. "You'd be my first priority, sweetheart, but I wouldn't rush it. I'd take the time to do it right, to make it perfect for you."

"You're really passionate about metadata," she sucked in a breath as his hands ran over her ass, down to the bottom of her skirt, "and hyperlinks."

Travis's nails lightly scraped the heated skin above her stockings. He pulled the twill fabric up for better access. His fingers slid easily across her arousal-moistened thighs, his lips curling upward at the discovery.

Her cheeks burned. Still, she opened wider. Shamelessly wanting more.

He snaked his fingers beneath the edge of her lacy bikini panties. Stroked her wet slit, back and forth without breaching her.

She rocked against his hand—an involuntary reaction—but he maintained the control, denying her the pressure and penetration she craved. Needed. One night with him and she'd turned into an addict, and only his personally delivered orgasms would do. She grabbed fistfuls of his jacket. Opened her mouth to beg, demand, something. All that came out was a gurgled squeak.

"Can I come over later—I promise to leave my idiot side at home."

The only word she registered from his request was *come*. "I'd like that." A whole big lot.

"Around six good?"

She managed an "Uh-huh" between breaths. Real speech was impossible with his fingers teasing her to the point of desperation. Her heavy breathing turned into a whimper when he withdrew.

"I'll bring dinner." He put the glistening fingers in his mouth. Sucked them clean, clearly savoring every second of it. "You can be dessert."

"Calli. Quit whatever you're doing and get down here." Caitlyn wouldn't be able to see them from the bottom of the stairs, but with the apartment door open at the top, and from the tone of her voice, she'd obviously heard them. "I have a mani-pedi appointment to keep. If I'm late, those women at Lucky Nails will start charging me for the extra topcoat."

"Five minutes," Calli called down.

An annoyed *hmph* floated up the stairs, followed by clacking heels.

"Your sister seems like... an interesting girl."

"She's really great, she's just not used to..." Nerves crowded her throat. Anything she said would sound cocky and presumptuous.

"To what?"

"Losing. Especially when it comes to men. Or competing with me."

Travis hugged her tight. His lips brushed hers with the softest kiss. "It was no competition. You're the woman I want."

Chapter Eight

Avoiding his computer wouldn't make the workload disappear. Neither would spending every free minute at Calli's place. Didn't see that changing, though.

He was completely into her, no question about it. Talking for hours, playing Scrabble—even when it wasn't the dirty version. Watching her eat strawberries—her favorite fruit—the way her lips wrapped around the red orb, sucking it into her mouth. That little appreciative moan she made while sucking the juice. His cock twitched thinking about it.

She never tried to be sexy, yet everything she did was erotic. He'd had four straight nights of kissing, licking and fucking her. Plus mornings, since he'd stayed over. Still wasn't enough.

Every hour he was here, away from her, was a chore. Focusing on work or music didn't keep his eyes off the clock, counting the minutes until she'd be done in the store. Not that she was going anywhere if he was late or didn't show. A lot of guys would kill to be in his situation. Hot girlfriend who was always available and eager to suck his cock, fuck him however he liked, but made no demands of him... score. He could pick up at the club tonight and she'd never know. She'd never catch him misbehaving because she never left her room—literally.

Wasn't going to happen though. In one week, being with other women had become the furthest thing from his mind. Now all he wanted was more time with one woman—Calli. Not just for the sex, it was more than that. Better. The sound of her laughter, the light in her eyes when she smiled. Knowing that he'd been the one to put it there did a number on him.

He was addicted. Spent hours thinking of ways he could make her happy. And her contented sigh when she leaned against his chest, the way her heartbeat settled into a steady, relaxed rhythm as she slept, safe and secure in his arms... Instead of bolting, he wanted those things. Wanted to be the man she counted on and trusted. A real connection. A future with somebody who stimulated his mind and soul, as well as his body. His gut said this was it, *she* was it. No way he'd fuck it up like he had the first night.

Exclusively hanging at her place was no big deal right now. Eventually, though, he wanted to take her out. To dinner and movies, on the road when they played out of town. Thinking about leaving her to go to the club tonight had made him realize that last part. He wanted her at his shows. Down in front or waiting behind the curtain, he didn't care. He wanted her there. That was a first that'd hit him hard. He'd fallen for Calli, and it wasn't just his cock doing the wanting.

He glanced at the digital clock next to his bed. Two o'clock. All he needed was a plan, a time management budget for the rest of the day. No problem. Work on this song for another hour. If he got back to the website project by three, he'd get two solid hours in before heading over to Calli's. Have a quick bite and possibly a quick something else with her, then be at the club by eight. Without her. Fuck.

Christmas, that was the target. One month to lure her out of that damn apartment and into the real world. Fully into his life. The band was booked for New Year's Eve—a popular venue in downtown Toronto. It would be a long, crazy night. No way he'd break away before midnight. On top of that was the hour drive, possibly in shit weather. He'd be lucky to make it to her place by the middle of the night at the earliest.

Not good enough. When the calendar rolled over to a new year, he wanted Calli's body pressed tight against him, those gorgeous eyes looking up into his.

Shit, if he didn't get his ass in gear and quit daydreaming like a teenager, it'd be time to swap his guitar for the computer keyboard. He cracked his neck side to side and slid his fingers up the fretboard of his Taylor acoustic. The steel strings hummed beneath his skin, the sensation as intrinsic as it was physical. Nothing beat holding a guitar. Almost nothing.

He closed his eyes and strummed the chords that'd been haunting his mind. Not the song he was supposed to be writing—a rock song with a catchy chorus for Black Box. This bit had floated up from somewhere else. And it'd come with lyrics.

I was drifting, full of empty space

Wishing for someone who didn't care about my face

A man with everything shouldn't complain, but that's exactly what I did

Until I read your words, looked in your eyes, kissed your lips

Yeah, this song wouldn't be on Black Box's playlist. And yeah, he had it bad for the woman inspiring it.

"Hi." Calli's gaze dropped to the case in his hand. "You brought your guitar."

"I could use an opinion about a song I'm working on, if you're willing."

"Oh—sure, I guess." She opened the door wider, making room for him to pass.

Not quite the enthusiasm he'd hoped for. Karmic payback for the times he'd refused women's requests to play for them. That novelty had worn off quickly, around the time he'd become a giant dick toward females in general.

Calli hadn't asked him to play. Not once, even subtly. The questions she had about his music or the band were business related, or about his training and how his interests had developed.

From her old CD collection and the library of MP3s in her laptop, he knew she listened to a lot of rock, folk and blues. Stuff he liked. Stuff he'd covered in clubs, like he'd be doing tonight.

"I'm finishing up in the kitchen," she said as they reached the door to her apartment. "Can I listen while I get supper on the table, or do I need to do something special—I'm not exactly qualified to give musical feedback, you realize."

Wrong. For this song, she was the most qualified person in the world. "You listen to what I've got and tell me what you think." He sat in one of her kitchen chairs and played. No singing, just the instrumental portion of the intro, verse and chorus, then the bridge.

She stood at the counter, arranging grated cheese on thick-sliced bread. She didn't look at him while he played, even though he couldn't take his eyes off her. Near the end, she tucked her hair behind one ear, giving him a view of her profile, including half a smile that made him bungle a chord. Shit.

"You wrote that?" Her normally throaty voice came out with a soft, silky quality that would've taken him down if he weren't already sitting.

"Except for that last note."

"It was beautiful. So... emotional. I love it."

"Calli, look at me." He had to see her face, all of it.

She took her time donning oven mitts—purple, of course—putting the bread in the oven and removing a casserole dish. Then she turned. She wore a calf-length denim skirt with a slit up one leg and a fitted, fully buttoned blouse, not unlike the one he'd destroyed during their first night together. Her dark hair pooled on one shoulder. A pink flush tinged her ivory skin. Could be the heat from the oven, but he'd bet not.

Every time he looked at her was like the first day—a yank on his heart, cock, brain and every other cell in his body. "If somebody were to ask me what it is about you that has me turned inside out, I wouldn't be able to answer."

"Gee, thanks, Travis."

She had to know what that did to him, hearing his name wrapped in her vocal caress. He'd certainly told her enough times. Showed her the effect. He leaned the guitar in the corner and crossed the short room to stand in front of her, caging her where she leaned on the counter.

"Because it's everything about you. Every inch of you on the outside," he nudged her head to the side to kiss her neck, "your intellect and sense of humor, your kind heart...the fact that you wear these shirts with a thousand tiny buttons." The top ones popped easily. Damn, she had the finest cleavage he'd ever laid eyes—or hands or tongue—on. And that skin-colored lace bra...Jesus. "And you drive me crazy with how sexy you are."

"I'm not sexy." Her breath hitched as he finished with the buttons, pushing the fabric aside to lick a line from her cleavage to her navel. "Other women are sexy. Like Caitlyn. Me, I'm—"

"Not even in the same category as her, sweetheart."

"I know. That's my point."

He looked up at her from his knees. Insecurity had stolen the blush from her face. "Your sister is attractive, but she works it way too hard. With you, it's as natural as breathing. Beauty, charm, sexuality—all without pretense. You're a fucking siren, Calli. How do you not know that?"

No answer. She bit her bottom lip and stared down at him.

Fine, he'd show her. Again and again, if that's what it took. He cupped her ass. Unzipped her skirt. Tugged it down and tossed it aside. Jesus god. Panties to match the bra. Nothing but see-through lace. No stockings today, just smooth, bare legs ending with dark-painted toenails.

He toyed with a braided ankle bracelet made from thin strips of leather and small beach pebbles. Her design. After she'd told him about her jewelry-making hobby the other night, he'd coaxed her to show him every piece she had on hand. They were incredible. Unique in subtle ways. Interesting enough to stand out without being overdone. Kind of like her. Whenever she talked about her handiwork or her business, she lit up. Confidence suited her. She should always be that way.

"This is nice." He spun the leather around her ankle, then ran his hands up her legs to the backs of her thighs. "I'd like to have one of your creations."

"I didn't picture you for an anklet kind of guy."

Funny girl. He shook his head and pressed a kiss to the lace between her legs. When she leaned into it, he added some tongue. Then her hands were in his hair. Teasing wouldn't cut it—not for either of them.

"Pretty panties, sweetheart, but they have to go." A little tug on the sides and the lace impediment disappeared. "You smell so good."

"That's the garlic bread." Her head fell back when he licked her. Slowly, deeply. "Or the pasta... cass... erole..."

The aroma of tonight's meal had set his stomach to a high rumble the second he set foot in the apartment. Calli could cook, had spoiled him the past few days with her culinary skills, but at this moment, all he wanted to eat was her.

He dipped his tongue inside her, scooped her essence into his mouth. Calli's taste went to work on him instantly. Her initial sweetness, the subtle spiciness that bloomed as she got more turned-on, drove him crazy.

He'd been at perpetual half-mast since the first day he saw her. The slightest touch gave him a full-on woody. But this—licking her pussy, devouring her like a starving man with a buffet all to himself—turned him to steel. Having his face buried between her legs was like being high. Better. Maybe because every drop of blood in his body raced to his cock. Maybe it was something deeper. He didn't care, just wanted more.

Above him, she moaned. Some undecipherable combination of words and gasps accompanying a tighter grip in his hair as she thrust her hips forward. Her thighs trembled against his chest.

Fuck, he loved when she got this way. Needy, wanting, uninhibited.

He leaned into her, securing her between his body and the cupboards. "I fucking love eating you." He suctioned his mouth over her clit, alternating between sucking and flicking until her whole body shook—then pulled back abruptly before she could finish. Jesus, her cry of frustration nearly made him lose it.

"Say it. Say what you want. Exactly what you want."

Her head lolled forward, that glorious long hair dangling above his head, framing her flushed cheeks and eyes that'd gone dark with desire. "Make me come, Travis."

His name again. His weakness with her—one of them,

anyway. A growl rumbled deep in his chest. "How?"

"Put your fingers in me and... suck my clit. I want to—" She bit her lip, then let it slide between her teeth, plump and bruised.

"Tell me." If she didn't spit it out in about two seconds, he'd dive back in there and finish her off, but fuck, he wanted to hear her say the words. "Anything, sweetheart. Anything you want."

"I want to... ride your face... while you... fuck me with your fingers."

All he needed to hear. He devoured her, suckling, lapping, driving his tongue against her clit. She moaned again, louder. Clutched at his head, pulling him closer, grinding against his face. Riding him while she sped toward her climax. His cock ached. His balls tightened into hot, hard rocks. Forget easy or slow, he pushed three fingers inside her pussy.

Her sexy voice filled the kitchen, "Travis, oh god... "

He relented only when she semi-collapsed atop his head. The pounding of her heart echoed in his ear. Her scent—that roses, soap and sex combo—surrounded him. Stripped his last inch of gentlemanly patience.

He eased out from her hold, grabbed a condom from his pocket and pushed his jeans and boxers out of the way. "You lick your lips once more while staring at my cock and I'm going to need you on your knees."

Wicked woman, she did it again, only slower and more purposefully.

Fine by him. He tossed the packet on the table. Shook his head when she grabbed a cushion from one of the chairs. "You won't be down there long enough to need that."

"In a hurry for dinner?"

"Only if you're it."

Sexy as hell in the open blouse and see-through bra, she knelt before him, her smiling face mere inches from his cock. She skated hands up his legs, nails raking the insides of his thighs. Palms splayed across his groin, she put those made-for-blowjobs lips on the head of his cock and sucked him inside.

He groaned and leaned into her. Pushed inside her welcoming mouth. Touched the back of her throat, felt her nose press against his stomach. God yeah.

Her moan hummed around him. Her eyes were closed, as they always were when she sucked him. The opposite of his—he had to watch. Take in every detail. Her eyelashes fluttering against pale skin, eyebrows drawn together in an intense little crease. Lips plump and shiny sliding up and down his cock. Cheeks hollowed from sucking him to perfection. So fucking beautiful.

Her hands drifted lower. One nail dragged over his balls, then back and forth along his perineum. Sparks shot from the source. Tightened his balls, sent more blood surging to his cock. Fuck, too good. Too close, too soon.

"Get up here." He choked the words out, grinning at her disappointed pout as she obeyed. "I fucking love it when you suck me."

"Then don't stop me. Let me do more."

He caught her arm as she tried to descend again. "Later." He snagged the condom and rolled it on. "Bend over the table and spread your legs. I want that sweet ass tipped up at me while I fuck you deep—as deep as I can sink my cock inside you." One of the things he'd discovered about Calli in their four nights together—she really got off on dirty talk. Hearing it and saying it, even when he had to coerce it out of her. And she took instructions *very* well. That sure as hell turned him on. Her too, from her responses.

Not that she was some shrinking submissive type. She had her own mind about things. Like taking her time stripping off her shirt and bra before assuming the position.

"That's even better." He slid his hands through the net of hair fanned across her back. "I love your hair. Love the feel of it around my fingers." He gave up touching her hair to smooth his palms over the creamy skin at her waist, the swell of her hips and ass. He parted her cheeks and ran one hand down the tempting valley, swallowing hard as he passed her puckered rosette. Not today, but soon.

She moaned when his fingers met her slippery heat. "Please..."

"Please what?" As if his control could endure more bedroom talk in her throaty tone. He must be a closet masochist.

"Please fuck me, Travis. As deep as you can."

"Fuck, Calli. I'll never last with you talking dirty *and* saying my name." One sweet stroke and he was balls-deep. He stilled, clenching his jaw. Fighting the pulse that threatened to end his ride before it'd started.

"Travis..."

Goddammit, was she trying to torture him? "Yeah?" He pulled back slowly, then slid in deep and fast. One hand on the middle of her back, he retreated and thrust again.

"I want you to-to—"

"To what, sweetheart, to what?" He'd be lucky to keep it together for another minute, max.

"Hold my hair and... pull."

He'd wanted to do this since their first time. With a flick of his wrist, the silky strands wrapped over his knuckles. Simply shortening the length had her head angled toward him. He tugged, just a bit. Enough to see the tip of her nose. He stroked into her tight body again, increasing the tension in his grasp, bringing the line of her delicate neck into view, causing her to emit a sound so raw and pure it undid him.

The last straw was watching her hands slip under her belly—that breathy gasp of pleasure she made as her orgasm mounted.

He needed to feel it—that perfect, slick heat blooming between her legs. He curled his free hand around her hip, then lower, twining his fingers with hers as they rubbed her clit. So much harder than he'd do it on his own.

"Do it. Again, harder."

She couldn't mean the rubbing, had to be her hair. He tugged again and she instantly responded, moving their hands frantically over her clit. Oh yeah, that was it. She arched. Moaned. Clenched around his throbbing cock.

"Sweet fucking hell..." Moaning and heavy breathing crowded his ears. One last thrust seated him deep, cock pulsing as he held her tight and captive against his hips. Face pressed to her hair, he came long and hard enough to damn near buckle his knees.

Burnt-toast smell infiltrated his senses. He opened his fist, letting the scent of her hair surround him. That didn't stop the smoke detector from wailing. Or the dog from howling in response. At least her apartment didn't have a sprinkler system.

"You're going to have to let me go," she said, wiggling beneath him.

There was only one way to answer that. "Never."

Travis had commandeered her clothing before dinner. When she'd deked around him en route to the bedroom, he'd caught her by the waist and wrestled her mock-protesting, one-hundred-percent naked body up against the wall.

"Don't cover up. I want to look at as much of you for as long as I can," he'd said.

When he said stuff like that, something grew inside her. A fledgling seed of confidence buried under years of being second best took root and pushed up the tiniest flower. So dinner au naturel it was. Sure, she'd eaten in her underwear before, what single person hadn't? But completely naked and in the company of a man—never. With Travis's knee brushing hers under the table and his smile mesmerizing her above the oak top, eating in the buff wasn't the tiniest bit awkward. In fact, it was hot.

Yet all they'd done was eat. The regular way, no cutesy

feeding each other bites of macaroni casserole, no lying bare-assed on the table and slurping cheese noodles from each other's navels. Not that those options hadn't crossed her mind. The way his eyes had stayed on her during their meal, darker than their normal light-hazel, he might've had some similar thoughts. But he hadn't moved one inch in her direction. Hadn't made a single double entendre. He'd talked. He'd eaten. One mouthful at a time, his strong jaw moving lazily as he chewed, with the occasional swipe of tongue over his perfect, chiseled lips added in for sensual torture.

By the time she stood to clear the dishes, she'd reached that state where one well-placed touch would be enough to send her over the edge. Again. This, after he'd fucked her with the heat and power of a volcano.

"You could come with me tonight. Watch from behind the curtain. You'd be ten feet away, in my line of sight." He stepped into boxer briefs that hugged him to perfection, making her mouth water. "I'd like to look over at my girlfriend while I play."

"Your girlfriend?"

Denim rustled as he shrugged the jeans up over nicely muscled legs. "Unless you're seeing somebody else. Because I'm not."

"You know I'm not."

"Good."

All kinds of warmth ran through her when he picked up her hands and tickled the tips with a kiss. Might've been the softness of his lips that did it. Or the deep smolder in his eyes.

"So you'll come?"

Despite the sweetness in his voice, the simple question stabbed at her gut. She didn't want to argue or defend herself—again—and she certainly didn't want to cry. She scooped her clothes into a ball. Let her hair crowd her face when she answered. "Give me a minute to use the washroom and I'll... walk you to the door, okay?"

"Sure."

The single word stung. What could've been one of the best moments of her life went in the crapper. Head down, she sidled past him, out of the room. She flicked on the bathroom light and stared in the small mirror. The bloom she'd felt earlier—gone. Withered and dull was all she saw in the glass.

"I hate you." Her reflection bounced the insult back. Most days she accepted who she was, the good parts and the shortcomings. Currently, she didn't feel so generous.

Music floated in from the kitchen—a few bars of the song Travis had played earlier. *To her.* Even without lyrics, there'd been no mistaking it for anything but a love song. God, what was wrong with her?

For the first time in years, she had a boyfriend. A gorgeous one with talent, brains and phenomenal bedroom skills. He wanted to take her out, the most natural thing in the world... and she was hiding in the damn bathroom, avoiding him.

She needed a grip. Or a kick in the ass. Both, concurrently.

The small medicine cabinet had three shelves that housed the usual suspects—toothpaste, toothbrush, moisturizers, tampons, bandages, Advil, etcetera. Her gaze settled on the brown pharmacy bottle that'd repeatedly failed on its promise of help. She popped the safety lid and shook an orange pill into her palm. It'd been a few months since she'd last tried the Alprazolam for her "panic disorder," as the doctor had labeled it. Maybe the medicine would work now that she had better motivation.

But what if it didn't? What if she managed to go outside with him, got all the way to his show, then lost it? It's not as if he'd be able to stop mid-song and take her home.

The strumming ended, the new silence punctuated by sharp clicks from the buckles on his guitar case. Footsteps followed, then his voice from the other side of the door. "Calli, I have to hit the road."

She dropped the tablet back into the bottle. "Coming."

"You okay?" he asked when she opened the door.

"Peachy as ever." Ugh, why was she being a sarcastic bitch to him—it wasn't his fault she was a headcase. "You know what, I'm not okay, but it's not your problem. I'm sorry." Thank god he didn't try to placate her with words. He just pulled her into a hug and let her melt there until she was ready to speak again. "Sometimes I wish I could go out at night for the convenience of it. But this, tonight," she sighed, tapping balled fists against his chest, "now I'm personally, royally pissed off at my stupid… limitations."

"So you want to come with me, but you don't think you can."

"Yes."

"That's all I needed to know." He kissed the top of her head before opening his arms. "Walk me out?"

They reached the back door too quickly, too quietly. Her chest tightened as he pulled on his coat and hat. Thirty seconds, sixty tops, and he'd be gone. Damn, damn, damn. Why couldn't she get over this?

Winter's chill filled the entryway. Travis stepped out to lean his guitar case on the back wall of the building. She moved up, right to the doorframe.

"I hope the audience likes that song you played."

"They won't hear it. It's not finished, and it's not for my band, anyway... it's for you."

Oh god. Pure emotion took over. She threw her arms around him, burying her face in his neck, soaking up his smell and warmth, memorizing, as if he were leaving for a month, or, forever. Tears threatened at the corners of her eyes. A stupid sob escaped, despite holding her breath.

"Bet you're rethinking that girlfriend thing now." Her words were muffled against his coat, as was his laugh against her hair.

"Not for a second, sweetheart." His arms closed around her and he lifted her off the ground. Rocked her a little, side to side. Then, they were moving, the sound of a door closing behind her.

Cold air rushed up her skirt, wrapping around her warm, bare legs. A small twist of her head gave her a view of their surroundings. "Travis, stop. What are you doing— I can't be out here."

"Shh, you're fine."

Good god, he'd carried her halfway down the alley. She blinked fast, desperate for her eyes to adjust to the darkness. Voices from the street out front stormed her ears—male voices. Her heart took off in her chest and her throat closed tight. She was absolutely *not* fine.

"Take me back inside," she said, burrowing into his coat.

"I will, in a minute. Just breathe. One deep breath at a time." He stopped and lowered her bare toes onto his shoes, inching her back from the safety of his chest. "Look around, look at me."

"Travis, please, don't."

"One look, that's all." He didn't let her go, but allowed more space between them. "Nobody will hurt you while I'm around, I promise you."

Light from the streetlamps taunted her eyelids. And the voices—how many were there? Were the men staring at her, laughing at the guy holding a crazy woman? Her mugger had laughed too.

"Trust me—"

"I don't want to!"

Travis stiffened. Without another word, he lifted her again. Carried her back to her door and plopped her down. For the longest minute they stared at each other across the threshold. Inches apart, in completely different worlds.

She wanted to say something to make him understand. Out there, in the dark, terrified her, even with him at her side. Inside equaled safety and control. When she opened her mouth, all that came out was fog against the cold. And when he grabbed his guitar and walked away, she felt anything but safe.

Chapter Nine

The venue was smaller than the previous week's, but you'd never know it by the noise level. They'd mixed rock covers with their own songs and the crowd had hooted, whistled and jumped to every single one. The energy from the floor had carried to the stage, energizing him—and the rest of the band, from what Travis could tell—to frenetic levels.

By the end of the second set, he was buzzing hard from adrenaline. Enough to follow Victor, Stubbs and Luke to the bar instead of heading out. Enough to knock back a couple of vodkas and order up a third instead of sticking to water and his precious fucking control.

Why the hell not, he had nowhere to be, nobody who *trusted* him enough to care what he did or why.

"Buy you a drink?"

Travis let his gaze wander over the woman who'd inserted her curvy body between his stool and Victor's. No denying her appeal. Legs that went on forever in painted-on jeans. Long dark hair streaked with chunks of red and blonde, shiny, full lips, long eyelashes, and a rack that'd make any man salivate. From behind her, Victor made lewd licking gestures, namely wiggling his tongue between the V of his fingers. Travis couldn't help smiling.

Miss Tall 'n Curvy must've assumed the smile was for her, and took it as an invitation to perch on his knee. Straddle his knee, actually. His leg heated under the press of her body. His dick went on alert, rising to the call of duty as she shimmied higher, closer. He lifted his glass and drained it.

"I'll buy you another, hot stuff. Vodka on the rocks?"

Another drink and he'd be looking at relaxed in the rearview, well on his way to stinking drunk. "Probably shouldn't."

"Ooh, a man who likes to maintain control, I like that." Her hand curled around the traitor in his jeans. "How about fucking—do you like to do that?"

Victor whistled and gave the thumbs-up, clearly approving that Travis was back in the game. "Travis is the king of fucking. I can attest to that personally."

The brunette swiveled enough to see both men. "Oh, is that right? I'm not coming between you, am I?"

"Not yet, but you could be." Wood scraped on the floor as Victor brought his stool closer. He palmed the woman's back, then slid his hand over her thigh. "What's your name, honey?"

"Honey works for me," she said, licking her lips at Victor while grinding onto Travis's quadriceps.

"Then Honey it is." Victor leaned in, close enough for Travis to smell the rye on his breath. "How 'bout we go to my place and get nice and sticky on my bed, the three of us."

Shit. This was getting way out of hand. Not to Victor, though—he was just getting warmed up. He'd caught scent of the player Travis used to be. Victor preferred that version, and looked intent on keeping him close. Very close.

"Honey, you and I are gonna curl up and enjoy some sixty-nine, 'cuz your lips look like they were made to blow me. And while I'm licking that honeypot of yours, my man Travis here is gonna fuck you from behind, maybe even in that pretty ass of yours, nice and hard like he likes to do."

"No." Travis ignored the blood that'd surged to his dick at Victor's description. They'd done that scene before. Other variations too. It'd been awhile, but his cock hadn't forgotten. "Just me."

Honey—whatever her real name was—pouted for a couple of seconds before blowing a kiss at Victor. "Tease me with that mustache next time."

"With pleasure," Victor said, then removed himself to scan the bar for new prospects.

"Didn't want to share me, huh?" She arched, pressing her half-exposed cannons against his chest. "I'm all yours now… what are you going to do with me, Travis?"

"Don't say my name." He jerked them both from the chair. Dragged her by the hand through the crowd to the small backstage room where the band had stowed their cases and coats.

It was too damn bright. He killed the lights with his free hand, then backed her against a wall.

"A little rough, huh, I'm into that. I'm into whatever

you want." Her voice was too high, her laugh too unnatural.

To shut her up, he pushed his tongue in her mouth. Without leaning down. Damn, she was tall. She tasted like hard alcohol, cigarettes and too much artificial mint. No good.

He cut the kiss, speaking before she had a chance. "Put that mouth to better use."

She dragged her nails over his t-shirt. On her knees in the dark, she clawed at his jeans until they were open, his cock filling her hand. "Travis, baby, you're gonna love the way I suck you down..."

His name in that high, nasally voice broke through. What the fuck was he doing? "Stop," he said, pulling away as her lips grazed the tip of his cock. He stepped back, stuffing his wayward dick in his pants and zipping. "We shouldn't be here."

A few seconds of denim shuffling forward and her hands were wrapped around his ass. "Ooh, we're gonna go get your friend from the bar and go to his place?"

He shook her loose and headed for the door. Hit the light switch and took another look at the woman he'd ordered to her knees. Attractive, willing. Plenty of women were. And none of them were Calli. Jesus, what had he done?

"Don't settle for shit like this, Honey. Guys like Victor and me, we'll treat you like a piece of meat. Use you. Fuck you 'til you're raw, shove cab fare in your pocket and laugh once you're gone. You can do better than us."

Her mouth was a gaping O. Maybe he'd shocked some sense into her. Maybe she'd go rub up against Victor and the other guys now that he was out of the picture. Either way, he was done.

From his position in bed, Travis could see a clear blue sky and more sunshine than he'd have thought possible on a late-November morning. Kersh purred at his feet instead of begging in his face. Last night's gig had netted him enough cash to do some serious Christmas shopping. Life would be good—if he hadn't screwed it up with that brunette from the bar.

He reread the texts from last night. Written proof of the damage he'd done.

After the blowup with Calli, he'd sat in his car out front of her building for twenty minutes he didn't have to spare, staring at her windows and his damn cell. A text, a call, her face peeking between the blinds. Anything. He would've been late to the club if it meant patching the wreck between them. But the only chirp from his phone had been Victor's message asking him when the fuck he planned on showing up.

So he'd given up. Assumed the worst, that they were done. He'd acted like an overbearing asshole, she'd countered by telling him she didn't want to trust him. After Victor's text, Travis had tossed his phone in the glove box. Hadn't looked at it again until he'd left the bar...five hours after peeling away from Calli's building, five minutes after coming to his senses in that backstage room. And too late to do anything about either one.

He scrolled to the first text she'd sent. If the timestamp was correct, she'd sent it about when he had a visitor to his lap. If he'd kept the phone in his pocket, he'd be in Calli's bed now, his body wrapped around a piece of heaven, instead of here in his self-inflicted hell.

I didn't mean that I don't want to trust you. Only that I didn't want to look around, like you'd asked right before that.

That's exactly what he'd thought when she yelled, "I don't want to". He'd been such a closed-minded, controlling idiot. Carrying her outside against her will to show her it was safe... Good intentions counted for squat if they scared the shit out of the woman he cared about. And from her next text, he'd done just that.

All I could hear were the men's voices, and even though you were right there, I was scared. I'm always so scared.

But her last text made his actions—all of them—even worse.

I trust you, Travis. I do. I hope it's not too late for you and me.

She trusted him. God damn it all.

He pressed his face to the pillow and groaned. Of course it was too late. Because he was still a self-righteous, womanizing bastard with a hot head. Same as he'd always been. Same as he would always be. He'd had a shot at something better—something incredible—with Calli, and he'd destroyed it in a week's time. Less. He'd been a dreaming fucking fool to think he could change, even for the right woman.

The phone chirped in his hand. He brought it closer, cracked one eye open to read the screen. A new message from Calli.

Are you still angry? If you are, I understand.

She couldn't possibly understand. Angry, yes. One hundred percent—at himself. It'd be simple enough to say nothing, but the guilt would eat him alive. What was he going to tell her when he saw her? That he was crazy about her, never stopped thinking about her, even when he'd been *this close* to shoving his cock down another woman's throat?

No, she deserved better than the shitty, sordid truth. She deserved better than a lie. She deserved better than him.

Not angry at you. I'll see you after work. He hit send on the message, muted the ringer and shoved the cell under a pillow. He had eight hours to come up with... something.

"You're acting weird today," Caitlyn said in a lull between customers. "Like you're hopped up on caffeine one minute, sort of a stoned zombie the next."

So it was noticeable. Great. "I'm, uh, taking the Alprazolam again. Hopefully those effects are my body adjusting to the medication, because that's pretty much how I feel."

"Oh." For a beat, Caitlyn stood and stared. Then she dropped the nightie she was straightening on a hanger and pulled Calli into a full-body hug. "Oh Cal, I'm so happy for you."

"Because I'm a jumpy, half-stoned zombie—thanks."

Caitlyn pasted a kiss on Calli's cheek. "Because you're

willing to be that way temporarily so you can get on with your life."

"I'm going to try. Don't get your hopes up, and for god's sake, don't tell Mom and Dad—or anyone—in case it doesn't work. Again."

"It'll work this time." The smile on Caitlyn's face couldn't get any smugger. "Now that you have some drop-dead-gorgeous motivation."

"Maybe." If she hadn't totally screwed up her chance with her hysterical fit. Travis's lack of contact last night and aloof, minimalist text this morning didn't leave her in the hopefully optimistic column.

Calli peeked at her sister, who'd returned to the business of tidying stock. As good a time as any to get some other stuff off her chest. "Hey, Cait…are you okay with me seeing Travis, since we sort of found him at the same time?"

"If I said no, would you stop?"

Since she'd already contemplated it, the answer was immediate. Just not easy to say out loud. "No, I wouldn't. I'd feel a little bad, but I'd keep seeing him anyway. Sorry."

A pair of sexy Santa undies hit her on the cheek, then fell to the floor. When Calli looked at the thrower, Caitlyn was smiling ear to ear.

"About time you grabbed ahold of what you want and refuse to let go. I've been waiting for you to wake up and realize how amazing you are."

All the years spent living in the shadow of Caitlyn's über-outgoing personality, thinking that's where Caitlyn, along with the rest of the world, wanted her. But Caitlyn didn't want Calli in the shadows. Neither did Travis.

This time the pills had to work. They had to.

She was alone in the store when Travis tapped on Romance U's picture window. Her heart picked up speed with each step closer to the door. Three doses of panic-disorder medication weren't going to make her instantly brave. But something was happening. The tiny beginning of a life-altering change, she could feel it budding, deep inside. Either that or she had the most monumental case of indigestion known to humankind. That would really be a sucky letdown.

She waved at him, enjoying the heat spreading through her body, warming her cheeks. Travis showing up on her doorstep always gave her a thrill. Today, the giddiness was different. Relief after what'd happened last night. Hope for what the nights to come might bring if the pills did their job. By the time she turned the deadbolt, her face threatened to crack open from smiling.

His expression didn't mirror hers. Not even remotely. There was no sexy grin, no sweeping her into his arms for a kiss. He looked like hell. Hell that edged by her without making a single point of contact.

"Your buzzer didn't go off when the door opened."

"Hi to you too," she said, locking up behind him. "It's still on the blink. The electrical panel looks fine to me, but that's not saying much. I've been too busy and too cheap to call a technician."

Business was steady, both in the store and online, but Charming's emergency vet bill had bitten into her savings. Renewing her prescription on a regular basis was going to take another big chomp. A downside of being an entrepreneur—no fancy drug plan, paid sick leave and such. Every penny counted.

Travis nodded. Because of his freelance work and the musician stuff, he understood that part of her life better than most. "I could take a look at it for you—I'm pretty good with electrical and circuitry."

"That's true." She gave his lapels a tug. "You always know how to turn *me* on."

The teensiest hint of a smile tugged at his mouth. Then it was gone. "I'll start with the panel, then open up the casing on the door mechanism if I need to. You have much more to do in here before you head upstairs?"

"I'm done, and you don't have to look at the door right now..." She wormed her hands into his coat pockets and found tightly balled fists. A bit of prying and they yielded—slightly.

"I'll feel better if I can get it working. Especially with those pervy emails you've been getting...since I won't be around to watch over you."

Something was off. Like, really off. "Tonight, or ever again?"

"As much. Some new web projects came my way, plus Black Box has weeknight gigs booked through the holidays. Some are out of town, meaning travel time." He freed his hands from his pockets. Took a half step back. "I'll be lucky to squeeze in some online Scrabble time."

Oh god, he was breaking up with her. Subtly weaseling

his way out of saying the words straight up, but this was unquestionably a breakup. The dark cloud hanging over him, the lack of kissing, his hesitancy to touch her at all...

"I get it. And, thanks."

"Thanks?" He coughed out a disgusted half laugh. "Don't thank me. I don't deserve it after—" His boot scuffed over the polished-concrete floor. Now he wasn't even making eye contact.

"After what happened last night? Is that why you're freezing me out, because you carted me outside against my will and I lost my mind? I reacted out of fear, Travis, but I'm not upset with you." She dared a step toward him. When he didn't move, she put her arms around his neck. Grabbing hold of what she wanted and not letting go, like Caitlyn had said. "Actually, it was a good thing. A wakeup call. You did me a favor, you big jerk, did *us* a favor. I'm going to try harder to beat this fear." She curled her fingers around his neck, bringing him down to meet her lips.

At the last second, he pulled up. "I kissed somebody last night."

"W-what?" Her arms went numb as they slid down his chest, releasing him.

"At the bar, after the show. A woman who made herself at home on my knee."

The image punched the air from her lungs. He'd kissed somebody else the same night he'd officially called her his girlfriend. After they'd had a huge misunderstanding, yes, one he could've assumed was a deal-breaker, relationship-wise, but still.

"Do you do that a lot, make out with women who throw themselves at you in bars?"

"I used to. You know that—I told you what an ass I've been."

That he had. He'd been brutally honest when they'd unpacked all their baggage during hours of late-night conversation. She'd naively believed him when he'd told her that part of his life was over. That he wanted it to be over.

"I wish to god it hadn't happened, that I could take it back. After our fight, or whatever it was, I didn't know what to think...that's no excuse, I know. I should've stopped things." He scrubbed his hand over his head, shaking it as he did. "I made a huge mistake."

She swallowed and nodded. Okay. It'd take time, but they could move past it. "Everybody makes mistakes. I appreciate you being honest with me...you didn't have to be, I wouldn't have known." Her hands shook where they wrung together in front of her. Her legs had started too. "We could go upstairs. Have dinner. Talk more, if you want."

"I can't."

"Because you have to be somewhere else, or because of what you did?"

"What I did."

Maybe forgiving him wasn't enough. She fought off the visual of Travis's lips touching another woman's, held her breath and stretched up to brush her mouth against his. Lightly, briefly. Then deeper, running her tongue along his seam. "I'll get over it, see?"

"It was more than a kiss, Calli."

"How much more?"

Hazel eyes pierced her straight through. "I told her to suck my dick."

Stability abandoned her. She stumbled backward, colliding with a rack, sending hangers with peignoir sets clattering to the floor. "And?"

"And she went to her knees, unzipped me and took out my cock. Then I told her to stop."

"Why'd you tell her to stop, so you c-could... fuck her instead? Tell me you used a condom."

"No condom—"

"Oh my god. How could you be so stupid and horrible and..." Her stomach lurched. "I think I'm going to be sick." She bolted, best she could around the tables and racks, to the two-piece washroom off her back office. The economy-issue sink groaned when she slammed against it. The first ripple of heaving took possession of her body, bile heating its way up her throat, though it didn't have the decency to make an exit. Tears were another story.

Light knocking rattled the door. "Let me in to help you."

"Go away."

"She didn't blow me and I didn't fuck her." This time he tried the handle.

"Stay out," she said, throwing her weight against the door when it opened a crack. Her five-foot-three, one-hundred-fifteen-pound frame was no match for a six-foot, muscular, determined man. From her experience in that alley two years ago, she knew this all too well.

Travis pushed in, filled the tiny space with his broad shoulders and broody demeanor. There wouldn't have been room to bend over and puke had she been able to.

"I'm not asking you to forgive me or understand. I don't deserve either one."

"Then why did you tell me… so you had an easy reason to end things with me?"

"That's the last thing I wanted." He pounded a fist against the doorframe, hard enough to vibrate the walls.

She shrank back, an instinctive response. Travis had muscles aplenty, she'd never doubted his strength or power, though all he'd ever been with her was gentle or sexy. He wouldn't hurt her. Her logical brain, her gut and heart knew it—her damaged areas did not.

"I'm sorry."

Sorry for scaring her, sorry for being unfaithful, sorry he'd told her at all? At this point, she wasn't sure she wanted to know the answer, so she swallowed the question.

"What now?" she whispered against the thick silence hanging between them.

A shrug accompanied his slow exhale of breath. "You deserve better than me."

"Meaning…"

"I leave."

"As in, no coming back?"

The lips she'd become addicted to kissing pulled to a

taut line. Hands that'd touched her all over, magically and skillfully, clenched into fists at his sides. "It's the only way to guarantee I won't hurt you again."

A large sob bubbled in her chest. "I'm not—asking—for guarantees." The words came between choppy breaths. So much for self-respect.

"Shit." He muttered the curse while wrapping his arms around her. His palms skimmed her back.

She pressed her cheek to the woolen coat keeping her from his soothing heartbeat. Thank god, oh thank god...

"I thought I could change, sweetheart. God knows I want to, but last night proves that I can't." His fingers moved to hers and began prying them loose. "The first sign of trouble and I fell back into being a prick. I've spent so long being that way, it's become my true nature. As much as I want to stay here with you, where I'm a decent guy with the most amazing girlfriend and the world is just about us, I can't. And outside of this bubble, I'm no good. Not for anyone, and especially not for somebody special like you."

No, dear god no. He held her an arm's length away while she failed to hold her emotions in check. Tears tracked down her cheeks. They dropped from her chin and nose, dotting her blouse like raindrops. Her breath hitched in short, shallow gulps. This is what she got for letting him in—into her apartment, into her bedroom and the worst spot of all, her heart.

"I should go, so you can—"

"Fall apart in private?" she bit out.

He groaned, removing his hand as he did. The last

contact—gone. "I have a buddy who's an electrical whiz and he owes me a favor. His name's Tom. I'll call him to come by and look at your door, see if he can get it working."

"Great." Her heart twisted at his relieved expression, the sharp edge of her pain morphing into a blade she wanted to poke him with until it stung. "Tell me, Travis," she said, hoping the use of his name would hurt, even if only a little. "Is your friend single? Is he hot? Does he like playing Scrabble, namely the dirty kind? Since I'm back on the market and all."

His eyes flickered. Anger, regret? Whatever it was disappeared as quickly as it had flared, leaving nothing but cool, deep hazel. "No idea, Calli. Guess you'll have to ask him yourself."

Chapter Ten

Saturday night had been rough. Sunday equally as bad. After using up all available tears, the anger had set in. Travis had said she deserved better than him, and damn it, he'd been right.

Yes, her panic disorder meant there'd be limitations in their relationship. But really, what relationship didn't have them? So what if she never went out after dark? They could've gone places during the day. It wasn't as if she'd asked him to stay in with her each and every night. He'd truly been an asshole. At least he'd had the decency to be an honest one.

At first, she'd been tempted to ditch the pills, curl into the fetal position and never leave her bed. Somehow, though, a scrap of hope had pushed through the rubble Travis's confession and subsequent departure created. That old saying that things will look better in the morning was bullshit, pretty much. The one about the wrath of a woman scorned, on the other hand... kind of on the money. She took the anger welling in her gut and aimed it at that feeble sprout. Travis or no Travis, she would fight her fear and win. She'd rejoin the world that existed after sundown.

Today was day five. She hadn't so much as fought back a sniffle—things were looking up. A good sign that her heart was on the mend. The pills were having an effect, and not just in the swinging-between-foggy-and-edgy-side-effect way. At nine last night she'd walked all the way to the lamppost with Charming. Without hyperventilating... too much. Only fifteen or so feet, but it'd been fully dark. A huge accomplishment, if she did say so herself. And yes, her first impulse had been to tell Travis about it. She hadn't given in to it—that was what counted.

"Hey, girl," Caitlyn said as she breezed through the front door for her evening shift. She stopped abruptly, hand frozen on the zipper of her stylish black leather jacket. "You look great today."

Calli understood it for the sincere compliment Caitlyn had intended. Another sign that things were changing, she was changing. Not too long ago she would've taken Caitlyn's comment the opposite way, dwelled on the negative—on the implication that most days, her gorgeous sister thought Calli looked like crap.

"Doesn't my sister look amazing?" This time, Caitlyn wasn't talking to her.

Calli's eyes lifted to the man who'd walked in. Tall but not ridiculously so, brown hair sticking out under a ball cap and a beard that bordered on bushy. Not ugly, but not a man she'd look twice at. Yet something about him made a blip on her radar. Maybe it was the way he looked past Caitlyn, the bombshell in the room, straight to the spot where Calli stood. He appraised her, every inch, before pulling the peak of his hat lower over his face. Embarrassed, was he? That was kind of endearing.

"Yeah, she sure does."

A compliment...about her. She'd take it. Especially these days. "Are you shopping for a holiday gift?" Calli asked.

"Uh, no. Not really."

Nothing new or unusual about this scenario, not to Calli or Caitlyn. Plenty of people came in to buy stuff for personal use. Easing customers through their initial discomfort at shopping for intimate items was an important part of the job.

Men were more difficult, in Calli's experience. Sometimes they left red-faced and empty-handed. Not until she'd given it her best shot, though. Starting with a verbal tour of the store and general information usually worked best.

"Clothing geared to the male physique is on the west wall. All of our feminine items come in a range of sizes that can accommodate most shapes and body types, and we've fitted *all* kinds of people, so don't be shy."

His eyes bugged out at that and she had to bite back a smile.

"Costumes, role-play gear, toys and accessories are in the rear of the store. Oh, and our glass is tinted so you can shop in privacy."

"Yeah, uh..." His eyes darted around, never landing on any product long enough to show a modicum of interest. The venting, windows and doors seemed to be more interesting.

Calli gave him a closer inspection for hints to his

character. Well-worn, tan twill bomber jacket, the kind you'd see on a blue-collar worker. Faded jeans with a smear of grease across one thigh. Work boots.

Of course... he was an electrician, the parting gift Travis had offered up for cracking her heart in two.

"Oh. Are you Tom, Travis's friend?" She let her shopgirl face relax and extended her right hand. "I'm Calli, his—" How to label herself... ex-girlfriend, one-week fling? "This is my store. I appreciate you taking the time to look at my broken door buzzer."

Something flickered in his brown eyes. He raised his hand, hesitated, then clasped hers solidly. "Yeah, that's me. Travis's buddy. Shoulda said so when I walked in. I guess seeing how pretty you are made me forget why I was here."

"No problem." Flattery was nice, but awkward coming from a guy who was friends with her ex. She smiled while trying to extract her hand.

Tom kept hold longer than necessary for a casual introduction, more firmly than appropriate for a man attempting a personal connection. A chill skittered along her spine before manifesting into a full-body outward shudder.

Now it was Tom who smiled.

Oh, that was just gross.

No big shocker that Travis associated with some less-than-charming types. If Tom could solve her technical issue, though, either for free or cheap, she'd grit her teeth through his creepy handholding and scrub her palm after he left.

"Did you bring tools, or...?"

"Tools, yeah. They're in my car. I'll go get them."

She released a long breath after the door closed behind him. Hopefully he'd pinpoint the problem and fix it quickly. Tom was definitely not a guy she'd invite to play Scrabble, not even an innocent game.

Travis's fury when she'd suggested she might hit on his friend so made no sense. He had to know Tom's demeanor would give her the willies. Maybe Travis hadn't cared as much as she'd thought.

"Hey, Cal, I think you should make yourself scarce while that Tom guy is checking things out. I didn't like the way he looked at you. Do you think Travis told him stuff about you—you know, dirty stuff?"

She couldn't picture it, Travis dishing out sex stories about her, especially not to a guy like this Tom. Then again, she wouldn't have pictured him being unfaithful with some slut in a bar. So, who knew?

"You don't mind if I leave you to deal with him?"

"Puh-lease," Caitlyn said, flapping a hand. "I've dealt with scummier guys plenty of times. Go upstairs and have dinner or whatever. I'll text you when the coast is clear."

"I think I'll take Charming out for a walk."

Caitlyn's eyebrows lifted. She glanced out the window, then back to Calli. "It'll be twilight soon."

"I can see that." The churning in her stomach sounded between them. Not fear, she wouldn't let it be. "Maybe I'll sneak him into the coffee shop and grab a sandwich too."

"Text me if you need me to lock up for a few minutes... if you get stuck out there, you know?"

Always willing to come to her rescue. How many people could count on their siblings the way Calli could? She squeezed Caitlyn's hand, an unspoken thanks for the support. "I will, but I won't."

Tom reappeared with a dirty cardboard box full of tools and a thin-lipped smile. Thousands of imaginary bugs crawled over Calli's skin. Thank god for her sister—again. In a way, thanks to Tom too, for creeping her out enough to leave the building with nighttime approaching. Motivation came in all kinds of packages these days.

"I have to step out, but Caitlyn can help you with any questions you have." She couldn't even lie and say it was nice to meet him. Ick. "Thanks for taking a look at the door."

By the time Calli plopped onto her bed, everything ached, from her toes that'd been crammed into fancy shoes for thirteen hours to her cheeks from nonstop courtesy smiling.

Tom had finished with the door—now back to its proper buzzing—and cleared out before she'd returned from her walk. Hallelujah on both counts.

The store had been packed with other people, though. The buying kind. Okay, not wall-to-wall packed like the big-name chain stores with their monstrous banners and buy-two-get-one-free promotions, but solidly bustling. A quick check of the email showed that the web store had been equally busy. All things seemed to be on the upswing, thank god.

Not surprisingly, Mr. Right Magnum Eight was a hit, especially online. Of the twenty-four she'd gotten in last week, she'd sold all but one. Well, two, if you counted the one in her top dresser drawer.

He was good to have around, Mr. Right, a real stress reliever. A friend in a time of need. He'd helped her get to sleep without crying twice this week. Any toy that could pull that off deserved his—*its*—five-star rating. Probably wasn't healthy to think of a sex toy as a *him*. Too much of that and she'd need a prescription for delusionism, if that was even a real word, let alone a condition.

She worked her blouse buttons free of their holes. The crisp cotton slid down her sides, tickling goose bumps to attention. Her nipples tightened inside the bra. The sensation in her breasts traveled a straight line to her core. No sex for years and she'd managed just fine. Then Travis had come along and stirred the pot, cranking up her libido a bazillion percent.

She trailed her fingertips across her midriff. Unzipped the side opening on her skirt and skimmed her fingers over the lacy front of her panties. The need for release tugged at her but it was too much effort.

If Travis were here, he'd divest her of these pesky clothes—kiss, lick and suck her until she didn't have a solid bone left in her body. Damn him.

Too beat to stand, she did the horizontal shimmy out of her pencil skirt and stockings. The bed was so soft beneath her, maybe she'd leave it at that. Close her eyes and sleep in her bra and undies.

No, she needed to haul herself to a sitting position and fire off an order to the supplier. If she sent it tonight, she'd be swimming in synthetic cocks by midday Monday. She giggled as she pictured it—her, sitting amongst a puddle of assorted dildos, maybe some fancy vibrators and colorful butt plugs for variety. God, she needed sleep, and bad. But she needed product more.

Little dog trotting at her heels, she dragged herself to the living room and cracked open the laptop. The preset windows opened in her browser—email and Wordloverz.

Travis had dirty-Scrabbled his way into her life only to resign the game. She hadn't called, texted or played with him since, but she always checked for him online. His avatar never popped up as available. The inactivity had given her hope the first couple times... until she thought on it more. If he wasn't online, he was probably out, playing his guitar for masses of adoring women. Or at home, fucking them.

But tonight he showed as logged in. Her pulse notched up. The red *invite* button might as well've filled the whole screen, such was its beacon-like effect on her. God help her, she clicked it, without giving it a second thought. So much for self-respect. Ditto for getting over him. Maybe he'd decline the game, cyber-hoof her to the curb, to go with the face-to-face dumping.

The site's virtual host appeared, holding a card that read, *Travis has accepted your invitation. It's your move.* The animated character winked at her, then slid off the screen, essentially leaving her alone with Travis.

Now what... play as if nothing had happened or logout

before she did something more foolish?

Travis leaned forward, his eyes glued to the screen. As if staring would make something happen, make some adorable comment magically appear in the message window. A minute ticked by. Maybe less, maybe more, either way, it felt like an hour.

He didn't deserve this game with Calli. Hadn't expected it'd ever happen. That hadn't stopped him from checking the damn website five times a day, every day. Now that he had her online, he didn't intend to let the opportunity pass. Even if that made him more of a selfish dick than he already was.

Your move, sweetheart.

No response popped up, but she hadn't left the game, either. Still hope. At least for the next hour's time.

He swiped his cell from the side table and brought up a picture. Calli sitting cross-legged on her bed, long hair covering most of her black bra. Her pretty eyes stared out of the phone at him. She had a bowl of chips in her lap and a fistful of cards. He'd suggested strip poker that night. She'd countered with strip Go Fish. They'd never finished the game but he'd definitely been the winner that night. All of the nights.

He scrolled through the shots he had—four she'd submitted to plus the two he'd snuck when she wasn't paying attention. She hadn't wanted him to take any. Not photogenic, didn't want to break the camera on his phone, she'd said. Crazy talk. He could've taken a hundred and it still wouldn't be enough.

Her opening move appeared on the board. *Dare*, for five points. Then a message to go with her pointed word. **Care to make the game interesting?**

Having you across the board makes this the most interesting thing I've done all week. Sucking up, damn right, but also the truth.

Somehow I doubt that.

Ouch. He had that coming.

Calli'd been willing to forgive his fuck-up. He'd refused, partly out of guilt, partly because he believed it would happen again. Wanting something different hadn't been enough to kill his old instinct to be a player. His behavior last Friday had made him think he couldn't change. And yet, on Saturday night, after Black Box's gig, merely looking around at the readily available women—and at Victor interacting with them—puke had risen in Travis's throat. Changing his ways was a choice. One he was ready and committed to make.

He was done. Truly done with that side of himself.

The tile gods were on his side tonight. He played *truth* and let the word speak in lieu of a message.

Still smooth, I see.

Not so smooth anymore. I quit shaving. He ran a hand over the bristly beginnings of a short-boxed beard. Son-of-a-bitch was itchy.

A little scruff is sexy, but don't let it get bushy and out of control like your friend's beard.

Like his friend's beard? Travis squinted at the screen.

He'd never shown Calli pictures of any buddies. And none of them had bushy beards. Even if she'd been looking at shots of the Black Box guys online, the only one with facial hair was Victor, and that was strictly a 'stache, no beard.

Maybe she was trying to make him jealous. It was working. The idea that Calli had been hanging out with any other guy, heavily bearded or otherwise, gnawed at his gut. Threw gasoline on his possessive-natured fire.

You hanging out with truckers and lumberjacks now? Travis waited, watching the stupid clock tick off four full minutes before typing another message. *Still with me?*

Sorry, thought I heard something downstairs. More craziness courtesy of my screwy brain.

His jaw clenched. He hated when she put herself down. His rat-bastard behavior had probably made it worse. The beard thing bugged him. And she still hadn't played a move. His brain was the one going crazy now.

Are your doors locked?

All six hundred deadbolts have been locked and double-checked, yes.

Cute.

Another message popped up on her side of the chat window. *Oh, and your friend Tom, the fuzzy-beard guy, fixed my door buzzer today, so thanks.*

His fingers practically flew over the keyboard. *Sweetheart, listen to me. None of my friends have that kind of facial hair. Tom's a six-foot-three baby-face. He couldn't grow a beard to save his life. Whoever it was who fixed your door, he wasn't a friend of mine.*

The hair on the back of his neck prickled. He stared at the laptop and its damn blinking cursor. Nothing. He set it aside and pulled on jeans and a t-shirt. Still nothing. "Damn it, Calli. Play a word, tell me to go to hell, do something."

He grabbed his cell. Brought up her number and hit call. Four rings, then her voicemail. He fired off a text. **Are you okay?**

No reply. That's it, he was out. If she laughed and slammed the door in his face, so be it. As long as he got to see for himself that she was safe.

He sent, *I'm on my way.* Headed for the door.

The temperature had plummeted since the sun went down. Frigid air stung his skin as he fought the wind. His Nissan protested when he turned the key in the ignition. Should've plugged in the block heater. He tried it again, holding his breath as the engine whined but didn't turn over. Not now, not fucking now. He pounded a fist into the steering wheel. Once more, then he'd call a cab. Take a bus. Run, if he had to.

"Start, you son of a—" Hallelujah. They had liftoff.

He swore at traffic. Ran two reds. Cut off a city bus and cringed as the driver laid on the horn. Hell, he would've tried to outrun the cops if necessary.

Finally, he reached her neighborhood. Then her street. Damn it, no spots in front of her store. The building was dark, but it didn't look as though there'd been a break-in. Not from the front.

He pulled into the narrow alley she used as a driveway, far enough to get off the street. The keys refused to be jammed in his pocket and fell to the ground, immediately swallowed by snow and darkness. To hell with them.

Front was closest, so he checked there first. Locked. He rounded the corner, past his car, down the alley to her back door. Also closed up tight. He pounded on the steel. Then the glass in the small window. Somewhere inside, Charming was barking his head off, going totally apeshit. But no Calli.

What the hell? He yanked on the doorknob—pointless with the locks she had in place. He put his boot to the door and called her name. Still nothing.

He had to get inside. Fuck it, he'd break a window. Not this one, he'd never fit through. He booked it around to the front. How was he going to bust through one of these plate-glass windows—drive his fucking car through it? If that's what he had to do. He jabbed his hands into his pockets—no keys. Because they were buried somewhere beside his car.

"Shit!" Could this night get any worse?

The distant, muffled scream from inside the building answered him. It could get a hell of a lot worse.

He tore around the closest side of the building, the unused one with the narrower laneway. And there it was, near the back and ground level—an old wood-paned window. He actually had a shot of squeezing through this one. Might get shredded in the process but they could stitch him up later.

He dropped to the ground, ready to kick the glass in.

The pane jiggled with the gust of air he created. Unlocked—from the inside. Fuck. He whirled around. Footprints in the snow that didn't belong to him. Shit. No.

He slid, legs first, into the small rectangular opening, having to shuck his coat to get his torso through and getting scraped to shit before the last of him cleared the frame. Some small good news—the guy who'd come through before him couldn't be any bigger than he was. And right now, there's no way that bastard could be more motivated.

The only light in the basement came from that window. He pulled his cell phone from his back pocket and swiped his finger across the screen. Instant flashlight. Thank god the room was tidy and mostly empty. He picked up a hammer lying on a storage container. Violence—hell yes, there'd be violence. He'd kill any man he found hurting Calli. And he wouldn't need the hammer to do it.

The springy wooden stairs creaked with each step. Hammer at the ready, he opened the door to the main floor. No sign of life in Calli's back office. Sounds, that was another story. A steady growl filtered under the bathroom door.

He ignored the door. Couldn't afford detection if Charming barked or bolted. At least the intruder hadn't killed her dog. That didn't mean he had the same code for the woman upstairs. *His* woman. The woman he'd started falling in love with during their first online chat, even if he hadn't realized it at the time.

He slunk through the office. The door separating the main-floor business from the stairs to her apartment stood open. No obvious damage to the door that he could make out given the dim lighting.

She always locked this at night, so what the hell? Their chat conversation ran through his head. She thought she'd heard a noise down here, then joked it off as paranoia. But she must've come down to check. Unknowingly opened the door to the bastard who'd entered through the basement window. Why had she chosen tonight of all nights to be brave? Damn it.

He paused at the foot of the stairs, beside the back door that opened to the small parking lot. This door was still locked up tight, same as the front had been when he'd tried it. She'd felt safe inside these brick walls, but all her damn locks hadn't protected her. He hadn't been here to protect her. Fuck.

One-handed, he worked the back door's deadbolts and slide-locks open, cursing silently at how much noise they caused. Think, be smart…tough to do when every cell in his body urged him to charge up the stairs. They needed the police, maybe an ambulance. Shit, he couldn't let his mind go there.

He slipped back into the office and hit 9-1-1 on his cell.

"9-1-1. What is the nature and location of your emergency?"

"There's an intruder at—"

Calli's choked-off scream ripped through Travis's sbody.

"The Romance U store, on Belmont, go to the back door," he rasped into the cell before dropping it. He took the stairs two at a time, calling out when he knew it'd be better to stay quiet. "Calli!"

No answer, nothing. Jesus, what if the bastard did something worse now?

The living room was trashed. Laptop smashed on the floor, cushions flung from the sofa, coffee table upended. No blood. Thank god.

Small apartment meant limited places for him to search—and for her to hide. Fury balled in his gut. He cocked the hammer and moved toward the bedroom. No light coming from the crack under the door. Shit, shit, shit. Calli's room was the black hole with the light off. He couldn't go in there swinging blindly. What if he connected with her?

"Yeah, go ahead and cry. I like that even more than the screaming." The male voice finished with a laugh. Then came the smacking of flesh on flesh. A whimper from Calli, a grunt from the man. And the unmistakable sound of a zipper.

"Get away from her, motherfucker," Travis hollered as he burst into the room. Not completely dark—the man pinning Calli to the bed held a heavy-duty Maglite, the beam illuminating Calli's bruised face before the intruder turned it on Travis, half-blinding him. Travis lunged in the man's direction, knocking the wind from both of them in a clumsy takedown.

He managed, "Calli, go," before the aluminum-barreled flashlight clocked him in the temple, then again in the jaw, filling his head with stars.

The bedside lamp flicked on, but everything was blurred. The guy jumped off Travis's chest. More screaming from Calli. A thud. Travis dragged himself to his knees. Blinked fast to focus. Jesus no. Calli was laid out on the floor, next-to-naked, pinned by a knife to the neck... and the fucker's pants were halfway down his ass.

A war cry whooped from deep in Travis's gut. He dove at the guy, rolling him off Calli, blindly pounding the piece of shit with blood-craving fury. He was going to kill the motherfucker.

"Calli..." Travis tried to sit up, but his body said *"fuck that shit"*.

"Shh, I'm right here." Her warm, delicate hand landed on his chest. "Oh god, Travis, I'm so sorry."

"For what, making me fall in love with you?" That's right, he'd said it. Said it and meant it. He struggled to smile at the big, soft eyes staring down at him. Face hurt too damn much. "I feel like shit."

"You got beat up pretty bad and they had to give you a lot of painkillers."

He turned his head and surveyed the room. "Hospital?" Shit, his head was like a fuzzy TV station. "Did they catch him?"

She pushed a chunk of hair behind her ear and nodded. "Yes and yes, thanks to you." Her left eye was swollen partly closed, her bottom lip puffed to twice its normal luscious size. A small bandage ran diagonally across her eyebrow. Another one near her collarbone. Little specks of black peeked out from beneath.

"You have stitches... he cut you?" His rage reignited at her nod. "I'll kill him. I'll kill him for what he did to you." He swallowed hard at exactly what that might be. "Did he—" The words refused to leave his mouth.

"No, you saved me from that. You saved my life."

Pain streaked up his side as he reached for the hair that'd fallen from its hold behind her ear. As he hissed at the burn, his eyes snagged on the state of his right arm. He must be damn drugged up not to have noticed sooner. "What the hell happened—I was on top of the guy, landing punches..."

Calli captured his arm, gently returned it to the bed. "He had a knife... and the hammer you dropped. You were getting the best of him until he stabbed you. The doctor said it didn't go that deep, that it missed all your organs, thank god, but there was so much blood..."

That explained the pain in his ribs, not the bandage and splints. "What about my hand?"

Tears rolled down her cheeks. "Two broken fingers."

"From the look on your face, I expected you to say they had to reattach it or something."

"You won't be able to play guitar for... months."

"Which two?"

"Middle and the ring finger."

Could be worse. Pieces of what'd happened poked through the fog in his head. The sharp sting of pain in his side. A throbbing sensation in his hand. Police appearing out of nowhere, weapons drawn, barking commands at the guy. That was pretty much the last thing.

No guitar for months. Probably the doctor being conservative.

"Doesn't even hurt," he said, lifting his right hand again, as if that proved a damn thing. "I'll be back at it in no time." He pushed his fully functioning left through her hair. Let the silk tickle his fingers before moving to lightly stroke her cheek and jaw. "See, my fingering hand works perfectly."

Her eyes opened wide and locked with his. "That *is* good news about your *fingering* hand." The sexy little smile budding on her face made all the cuts and bruises invisible. So beautiful. And still dirty-minded, despite the horror she'd just been through.

"Want to get in bed with me for a demonstration?"

"They don't make hospital beds for two, Travis."

Now she'd done it, addressing him by name. The drugs they'd given him might be numbing his pain, but they weren't affecting his cock. "That's not exactly a no."

"Hmm. I think we've played this game before."

That, and better. He tipped his head at the sliver of bed to his left. "I dare you."

"Shouldn't I get a choice of truth or dare?"

Either way, he'd win. "Sure, sweetheart. It's your move, pick one."

"Truth."

He ignored the ache in his jaw and smiled. "Do you

want to get into this bed with me?" He expected hedging. It didn't happen. She didn't even answer. Simply walked around the bed and slid her body along his left side. He didn't shift to give her more room, just curled his good arm around her and dragged her half on top of him.

"I hope I don't hurt you," she said.

"If you do, it'll be worth it." He'd missed the way she looked into him—not at him, like most people, most women, did. When they left this room, it had to be together.

Her toes slid up and down his shin, her warm thigh pressed firmly against his quad. Soft skin on his scruff. Lots of it.

"I have a new appreciation for hospital gowns. Easy access is my friend." He undid the tie at the back of her neck with a lazy tug. Traced her spine to the bottom, palmed the high curve of her sweet ass. "Is this okay—do you have any sore spots I can't see?"

"No, my face got the brunt of it. Thank god it's kind of dark in here... I'm not exactly easy on the eyes."

"Hey..." He stifled a wince while reaching to tip her chin with his right arm. "You're still the most beautiful woman I've ever seen. The only one I want to see."

"Those must be some good drugs they shot into your cute butt."

"Let's find out."

"What do you want me to do, poke you in the stitches, step on your splint?"

Laughing hurt, but he did it anyway. "Not quite what I had in mind." He brought her hand to the tent pole holding up the flimsy hospital bedding.

"Am I supposed to be checking for damage?" she asked, sliding her fist up and down his length.

A week without Calli's touch had been hell. Some kind of answer gurgled in his throat, making her giggle. One of the best sounds he'd ever heard.

The crisp shuffling of sheets seemed loud against the silence. Calli's "mmmm" as she licked his cock, base to tip, even louder. Only his groan when her tongue teased the slit, lapping the pre-cum, topped it. Then her lips closed over the head of his cock.

"Sweetheart, your mouth..." Had to hurt like a bitch with that swollen lip.

"Is in heaven," she said without fully releasing him.

"*Feels* like heaven." He tried to be still so she could take it slow. God, he tried. Until she reached up for his left hand and moved it to her head. "Shit, I can't. I'll hurt you."

She answered by folding his fingers around a chunk of her hair. A better man would've pulled his hand away, not closed his grip. Not given in to his urges.

The sight of her hair wrapped around his fist sent a warning swell to his groin. "Sweet Jesus, Calli, stop." But she didn't stop. Instead, she looked up through the fringe of bangs, moaning around his cock as their eyes locked. He knew that sound, that heavy-lidded look. Knew that her hand was between her legs, that the second her eyes closed, she'd gone over.

Anything—he needed to think about anything other than how good it would feel to come in her warm, welcoming mouth.

"You didn't come…" Her voice held a pout that rivaled her face. "Was it because I couldn't suck as hard as usual?"

He used his good hand to pull her up to the pillow. "God no. It took every ounce of willpower to hold back. I want to be inside you the next time I come."

"Now, here?"

"I was thinking after we went home, but now works for me. I love smart women with good ideas."

"Travis, we can't… it'll hurt you and… we don't have anything."

She expected him to hold off after whispering his name—while pulling on his cock? Not happening. And if she didn't lay off the tugging, about sixty seconds from now they weren't going to need anything.

"Is my stuff here?" He breathed a sigh of relief at her nod. "In my wallet."

Calli tiptoed past the empty bed beside theirs to a closet. Only she could make a hospital gown adorable and sexy. A minute later she crawled back onto the bed, foil packet in hand.

"You're going to have to do it," he raised his injured hand, "kind of out of commission here."

Gingerly, she tore the package. She handled the condom as if it were something precious, rolling it down over his shaft with a reverence that stoked his possessive instinct.

"Lose the gown—I want to see all of you."

Her hand toyed with the fabric on her shoulders. "Somebody might walk in."

"That's not exactly a no," he said, and she giggled. The sweet sound echoed, and for the first time since he'd woken, he noticed the silence surrounding them. He'd been unconscious for god knows how long. Knocked out, drugged out, then sleeping it all off. "What time is it?"

"Around four."

Four in the morning. Holy shit. "Wait... how'd you get here?"

"Ambulance, same as you."

At night, in the dark. Anger readied in his gut at the possibilities. "Did you tell them you couldn't go out? Did somebody make you?" He jerked forward to sit up—only to have a stab of pain in his side insist he lie the fuck back down.

"Shh... The paramedics said I needed a full examination, maybe x-rays or a CAT scan, but nobody had to put the white jacket on me. I came willingly."

"I like it when you come willingly."

She crept up the bed, over his legs. "You're pretty quick for a man who's been stabbed, beaten and heavily sedated."

"Not that quick, I have to see you come willingly first."

"I already did… guess you missed it."

"I saw and I enjoyed. But I'm a greedy man—I want to see it again."

She straddled him, hovering above his cock, teasing him with small passes. But the damn hospital gown blocked his view. Not good enough. He pulled the material from her body and let it fall to the floor. Better. Even if he couldn't lean forward and nibble her nipples, he could appreciate them visually. Touch them with his left hand, roll the hard points between his good fingers.

He let his hand slide down, dragging his nails over her skin the way she liked. The goose bumps popping up all over were reward enough. Her smile, the shine in her eyes as she sank onto his cock—those were the erotic jackpot.

"Is this okay?" she asked on a slow downstroke.

"You're riding my cock, it's a hell of a lot more than okay."

"And you're talking, not even breathing heavy, so I know it's barely passing for okay."

"You're right, we can do better than this." He fumbled around until he located the remote some nurse must've clipped to his pillow. "How do you raise this thing…?"

Calli leaned forward to work the controls, putting her tits directly in line with his mouth. Not an invitation he'd pass up. He caught one in his mouth. Circled the nipple with his tongue, then sucked at the peak.

Soft whirring from the bed's motor drowned out the sound of Calli's pleasure. He didn't need to hear it. Her back arched. Her hand clenched on his shoulder, her fingers curling into his muscles. And her hips—Jesus—her hips rocked and rolled over him, swallowing his cock again and again. Deeper, harder.

A soft moan filtered down to his ears. Then skin smacking. She ground against him, her whole body shaking. He slid his good hand between them and found her clit.

"Oh god, Travis, I, oh god... "

Hearing his name in her sexy voice, her body bucking against him, squeezing his cock as she went over—he was done for. He thrust up to meet her writhing body. Pinned her hips in place and gave in. "Fuck, so good, you feel so good."

"Oh!" The single-word exclamation hadn't come from Calli's perfect lips. A nurse stood in the now-open doorway.

"Oh my god." Calli's eyes flickered to the remote still clenched in her fist. The bed and his cock weren't the only things she'd raised. "Oh shit." She scrambled off him, yanking the sheet up as she went. "I'm so sorry, I must've hit the—damn it, where's my stupid gown?"

He was probably going to hell for laughing. If not that far, definitely to Calli's doghouse by the look she shot him.

"At least you didn't call for a Code Blue team," the nurse said once Calli had restored her modesty with the flimsy gown. "Now *that* would've been embarrassing."

Thank god for a nurse with a sense of humor.

"Bet you've seen it all." Travis worked the condom free and stuffed it under the pillow. Nurses didn't fluff pillows, did they?

A smile ticked at the woman's mouth. Hard to be sure in the dim lighting, but she looked about fortyish, and not the hard-ass type. At least, until she reached the bedside.

"I understand the need to physically connect after a traumatic experience, but you two have made a real mess here." She shot Calli a pointed stare. "You'll have to excuse us, please. Mr. Graham needs his wound cleaned... and new stitches."

Calli leaned over the bathroom sink for a closer look. Four raised red dots decorated her eyebrow. They'd fade with time, she knew from experience, but there'd always be four tiny scars. She let her bangs drop into place. There, hidden.

She turned her attention to the similar marks on her collarbone. The cut on her forehead had come from her assailant's fist. The one near her neck was from his knife. A small slice, no more than an inch, it'd required four stitches that'd left eight red spots. Good thing she liked polka dots.

Aside from testifying in court, she was officially done with the horror of the last two years. Jason Barros was in custody and destined to remain there for a good long while. Unlawful entry, assault, assault with a weapon, attempted rape. The police had even charged him with attempted murder. And those were from the recent encounter.

After searching Barros' apartment, police had added a string of charges for the mugging incident two years ago. That explained the weird familiarity she'd experienced when he walked into Romance U. He hadn't had the beard or the baseball cap back then and it'd been dark. Still, she should've recognized him, shouldn't she?

Apparently, he hadn't been satisfied with beating the shit out of her and taking her money. The police told her Barros had likely traced her from the bank deposit slip— it'd been pinned to a bulletin board in his bedroom, along with photos he'd taken, ads for her store and handwritten lists of information he'd gathered—somehow. Scary, the stuff he knew. He'd been behind the progressively creepier emails she'd been getting too. All the pieces fit together in one horrific puzzle.

For two years he'd been hanging back, waiting for the opportunity to finish what he started before she'd lost consciousness in that alley. Her fear, the thing that she'd hated for controlling her life the past twenty-four months, had probably saved her. That, and Travis, her honest and true hero.

Travis. She hadn't seen him since the intense encounter that'd blown out seven of his stitches. The nurse had commanded her out of the room while they repaired him. Calli hadn't gone back. God, she'd wanted to. So much, the ache of it hurt worse than the cuts and bruises Barros had given her.

After pacing the gray linoleum for hours, waffling between returning to Travis's room and crying into her hospital-issue pillow, she'd just signed out. Called Caitlyn for a lift and gone home. Hidden. Thrown herself into scrubbing the apartment, the store, even the basement, scouring every surface until anything Jason Barros might've touched was sanitized. Then she'd focused on the impending Christmas rush at work. Anything to prevent *calling* Travis. Hearing his deep, sexy voice would've crushed her resolve to let him go quietly. The last thing either of them needed was another ugly scene.

They'd had one amazing week, connected in ways she hadn't dreamed of. Not only had he given her a reason to chip away at the fear, he'd literally saved her life, for god's sake. And that night they'd shared in his hospital bed... just, wow. He'd said he'd fallen in love with her. But. Yes, but.

None of those things would've mattered once reality set in. And it would have. It might not've happened in the hospital, but once Travis was released, dealing with a gimpy hand and *not* playing guitar, he'd have resented her. Maybe hated her.

A musician unable to make music... might as well tell the man he wasn't allowed to breathe. Not to mention the hit to his bank account for all the lost shows. The damage to his budding career. His band-mates had replaced him—he'd told her that much in his texts. Temporarily, she'd assumed, until she went to Black Box's website. Travis's pictures and bio... gone. *She'd* cost him that. How could he *not* despise her?

She couldn't bear another heartbreaking goodbye. Equally as bad, the thought that he might come around out of pity or concern. She wouldn't put either of them through those options.

So she'd kept communication to safe subjects. His recovery. His plans. He'd answered her texts, inquired about the case and her condition, but it'd ended there. Not once had he asked to come over. Called. Stopped by the store. Mentioned their last night together. The texts had gotten more awkward than having sex in a hospital bed.

She'd sent her last yesterday. A few lines, simple. Letting him know that she was okay, physically and mentally—her way of absolving him, should he have any lingering tendencies toward duty—and telling him she planned to live her life to the fullest, reclaim it now that Barros was behind bars. This time, he hadn't replied. No reason he should.

So it was over, again. Calmer this time. Sadder too. She was ready to move forward, finally, make life an adventure instead of a sentencing. Unfortunately, the man she wanted along for the trip wasn't interested in claiming his ticket.

Chapter Eleven

Calli rolled the last blown-glass ornament in tissue and tucked it amongst the rest. She snapped the lid on the storage tote. Christmas, officially packed away for another year. Some stores tore down their holiday decorations before the New Year hit. She preferred to let hers linger until the end of January—had never understood the desire to put such a happy season away in a big hurry.

Four forty-five, according to the wall clock. Not closing time for fifteen minutes yet, but the boom, such as it was, had long since passed. If another person walked through the door she'd be shocked. More so if she or Caitlyn made another sale.

She really didn't need Caitlyn's help at this time of year. Paying her to hang around ensured that her sister wouldn't take a job elsewhere, so it made sense, business-wise. The company was nice too. Helped keep Calli's mind off Travis. For a few hours, at least.

"I think it's safe for us to call it a day."

Caitlyn's jaw dropped in true dramatic style. "My fiscally motivated sister locking up early on a Saturday... am I on one of those hidden-camera shows?"

"We haven't had a customer since three o'clock." She flipped the door sign and turned the locks. "I'm sure you have better places to be on a weekend."

"Uh-huh." Caitlyn's patent-leather boot tapped on the floor. She'd obviously scented a story. "And you—what plans do you have? Read a book, watch a chick-flick… call an old boyfriend like you should've done weeks ago… "

More *gentle* encouragement about Travis. The only way to get Caitlyn to give it up was to show her it was no longer necessary. "Actually, I do have a date—with Joe."

"The guy you met at the coffee shop?" Caitlyn threw her hands up when Calli nodded. "That's probably not even his real name, Cal. I mean, really, what're the odds you'd meet a guy named Joe at Cuppa Joe Coffee House?"

"Joseph is a very common name. Tenth most common the year he was born." Okay, that kind of gave away the fact that she'd Googled him backward and forward. Oops. "He's nice. Average. Totally nonthreatening."

"Sounds like an exciting guy," Caitlyn said with a snort.

"Exciting guys aren't my type." Not a lie, since she'd used the plural form of guys. One exciting guy was her type, but he was off the menu.

"Where're you going—do you have me programmed as your emergency call number, in case you… have a setback?"

"You mean should I flip out and need to retreat to my hidey-hole," she said on a laugh. God, it felt good to be able to laugh about it. So far, the nighttime outings she'd attempted had been successful. Short, purposeful errands to familiar places. A social outing was next on her list, but not with some guy she barely knew. She wasn't that brave yet. "He's coming here. I have chicken in the Crock-Pot and James Bond queued-up for later."

"No Scrabble?"

"Definitely no Scrabble." Travis had ruined her for other men when it came to Scrabble, even the innocent kind.

Caitlyn's eyebrows pinched together. "Text me after he leaves, so I know you're safe."

"I'm fine, honestly. Jason Barros is in jail. I'm taking the Alprazolam and seeing a counselor once a week. And Joe's a decent guy. He's aware of my issues and says he won't pressure me."

"Does he know about the issue where you're in love with somebody else but too stubborn to reach out to him?"

"It's dinner and a DVD, not a marriage proposal. How I may or may not feel about somebody else is irrelevant." That's the closest thing to an admission she planned to give. They could discuss the Travis situation for hours, and had, to no useful end. That story had ended. Just not with a happily ever after.

"Okay." Caitlyn pulled her into a full-body hug, complete with extra squeeze, then let her go. "Look, I want you to be happy, hon. If coffee-boy can do that for you, I'll stop harassing you about T—your ex."

Travis flexed his right hand, curling the fingertips tight to his palm. A habit he'd developed since physiotherapy. He'd cursed in the therapist's face the first time she manipulated his fingers to this position. Such a small, everyday movement—one he'd taken for granted until he lost it. It'd been real work getting his newly knitted bones to bend the way he wanted them to. Needed them to. But he'd done it.

And now he had another booking lined up. Small place, he'd be playing for maybe seventy-five people, tops. Still felt great. A fresh start, or some shit like that.

He shook the manager's hand and walked out of the office. Tonight's act was settling in on the small stage. One guy with a guitar and a microphone—like him, now that he was a solo act. Nowhere he had to be... might as well grab a seat at the bar and listen to a set. Check out the new competition.

"Iced tea," he told the bartender who wandered over. The frosty glass numbed the ghost of an ache in his middle finger. Nothing he couldn't deal with, still, he'd be happy to have it gone, permanently.

Loud rumbling shot from the speakers when the on-stage guy cleared his throat into the mic. More noise as he fumbled with the microphone stand, bumped into the piano.

Travis gritted his teeth. The guy was either nervous or oblivious. This wasn't some club filled with hundreds of loud voices and thumping background music—it was a bistro that featured live entertainment, not headliner acts. Yeah. Quite a step down from the Black Box gigs.

Step down was too generous. Black Box was a signature away from a recording contract. Pretty soon they'd be touring, opening for big-name rock bands. And he'd be a one-man show, playing for restaurant patrons, half of whom probably wouldn't notice him sitting on the rinky-dink platform, pouring his heart into his music.

He snorted. Good thing he wasn't bitter. But he'd made his decision, now it was time to move on.

Dude with the guitar started playing. Didn't bother to introduce himself or address the patrons. No-name up there needed a few lessons in marketing. Music was pretty good though. Instrumental. A little bit slow, a little bit sexy, sort of a Spanish flavor. The kind of song a couple could dance to, nice and close. And one did, in the small space bordering the stage.

Hard to judge their ages from this distance. Late thirties, early forties maybe? Irrelevant. It was their body language that mattered, kept his eyes glued to the spot where they swayed.

Twenty-five feet away and he could practically feel the chemistry. The woman had to tip her head back to look at her partner. Like Calli did with him. The dancing woman's smile suggested whatever was coming from her partner's moving lips was a very good thing. The man held one of her hands in his, tucked between their chests. His other hand rested near the top of her ass, palm flattened for maximum contact. Holding her where he wanted her while simultaneously letting every man in the place know that she belonged with him.

Which led his mind back to Calli. Not that it ever strayed too far or for too long. That one week together that'd changed everything for him—made him want the white picket fence, or whatever their version of that fairytale might've been. His screw-up in the bar, the attack, what he'd thought was them getting back together in the hospital. But then she'd disappeared. Taken off without a goodbye. Sent him a handful of polite texts that never touched on the topic of *them*, as a couple.

And that last text, fuck. He pulled out his phone and brought it up on the screen. Ground his teeth while reading. Again.

Travis... Just wanted you to know that I'm okay. My stitches come out tomorrow and the bruises are almost gone. I'm okay upstairs too. Not just in my apartment, though I did have the locks changed and scrubbed the place sterile, but upstairs meaning my head. It's time I reclaimed my life, lived it to the fullest, so that's what I plan to do. I hope that somewhere inside, you'll be happy about this. I wouldn't be here—literally or figuratively— without you.

If that wasn't a Dear John text, he didn't know what the hell was. He hadn't bothered to reply. To say what? Have a nice life? He wanted that for her, only with him along for the ride. To beg for yet another chance? Yeah, she'd want to give him that... not.

It'd been two damn months since he'd seen her. Still couldn't shake her from his system. Every day was a battle *not* to do something. Call her, text, check the Wordloverz site to see if she was logged in. He found excuses to drive up and down her street, as if that'd do anything. Yet he kept doing it. He'd traveled that stretch of asphalt more in the last sixty days than he had in the five years beforehand. Lovesick idiot—that was him.

Only an idiot would've screwed up a second time. Taking advantage of her heightened emotional state in the hospital... what the hell had he been thinking? He could try passing it off as the drugs they'd given him, but that'd be bullshit, not to mention a cheap excuse.

He'd wanted her—needed her—and made it happen. Hadn't taken the time to talk things through, to grovel for his sins or make sure she was okay, deep inside, after everything she'd been through. The mess he'd made between them. Barely escaping a vicious attack.

Then that nurse had walked in. *He* could've shrugged it off. He'd had an audience to a hell of a lot more compromising situations. Sometimes by choice.

But Calli hadn't. She was sensual and uninhibited, but that didn't make her an exhibitionist or a woman who took sex lightly. And it hadn't been a casual fuck. Not at all. To him, it'd been a new beginning. He certainly hadn't wanted to get caught, but he wasn't ashamed of it, either. Caught making love with the one woman he was crazy about—no shame in that. Hell, one of his first thoughts had been that years from now, they'd look back on it and laugh. Only there wouldn't be a *years from now* for them.

If her mortified reaction hadn't made it clear enough that a dirty dog like him didn't belong with a woman like her, her absence after the fact made it crystal. She'd left the hospital without a word. Not even a note.

Sure, she'd texted in the days that followed. Each one came with an apology and questions about his physical recovery. Guilt. He got that. Could've used it to worm his way back into her life. Hadn't. When that last message had come, he'd done what needed to be done. The best thing for her was to let her go.

So why was he standing in an alcove near the restrooms with his cell to his ear? Because underneath his good intentions, he'd always be a selfish bastard, that's why.

"Hello?"

Damn. That voice, sexy as ever. "Hey. It's Travis."

"I know, I saw on the call display."

"And you answered anyway." Shit, he wasn't off to a great start here.

"Of course I did... I'll always answer your call, Travis."

He let the sound of his name in her throaty whisper wash over him. One word. Still did things to his insides. And his outside, enough to require he shift his thickening cock.

"How—how are you? Is everything okay?"

He should say yes, ask her the same, then end the call. "No. I'm in a restaurant, alone, watching this couple dance to a slow song and missing you so much it's—" Crazy. Was he crazy, or had he heard a guy's voice in the background? "You have company."

"Uh, yes."

"Your dad?"

Silence. Too many seconds of it.

"No, a friend."

He curled his right hand into a tight ball. "I shouldn't have called."

"I want to talk to you, but now isn't a good time."

"Yeah, I bet."

"Travis—"

He pounded his fist against the wall. Pain shot through his fingers. "Fuck. *Fuck.*" He flexed his hand, wincing at the throbbing pulse working its way up his arm.

"What happened—are you okay, do you need help?"

"What if I do... you going to jump in your car and come rescue me this time?" Cruel, but he had to undo the mistake he'd made by calling, spilling his guts. "I don't need rescuing, sweetheart, just another Absolut on the rocks."

"You don't drink."

"Didn't. Things change, right?" What difference did it make if he lied now? "Have a good night with your friend." He stuffed the phone in his back pocket, ignoring it when it rang immediately.

She'd moved on. He should be happy for her. Nope, couldn't summon an ounce, only raw jealousy.

Feminine giggling jerked him out of his black cloud. Two young women, a blonde and a brunette, both hotter than habaneros, eyeing him up as they made their way to the restroom area. A couple lines of small talk and he could probably take one home. Maybe both.

"Ladies," he said with a nod, then walked away.

"Lock up, would you, I'm going to do a read on the till." Calli ran the daily sales report, eyes bugging at the numbers. "Holy crap, Cait, we sold as much today as the Saturday before Christmas."

"Love is in the air. That, and the promise of hot

Valentine's Day smexing." Caitlyn stood, hands on hips, surveying the disastrous state of Romance U after their banner day. "It looks like the place has been ransacked— by dozens of horny men and women."

Calli laughed. That about summed it up. "Let's leave it until tomorrow."

"Whoa. You feeling sick, boss? You never leave the store a mess. *Never.*" One perfectly waxed and shaped eyebrow rose, the knowing expression aimed directly at Calli. "You're planning on bailing. I'm onto you, Cal. You think you're going to wiggle out of our plans and spend Valentine's night cleaning the store."

Busted. "Yeah, about that..." A handful of panties bounced off her blouse.

"Start folding. You're coming with me tonight. No bailing, no wiggling. Not this time."

"I'll go next time, I swear."

"Great. But that doesn't change the fact that you're going tonight."

Half the table was already in order—Caitlyn's half. The woman was a panty-straightening machine.

"It's Valentine's Day. You should be hooking up with some hottie, not dragging your pathetic sister out for an unromantic dinner."

"Since I don't have one of those, I'm not."

"You don't have a hottie on the go? That's a first."

"Nice. You make me sound like a man-eating slut... which I am, more or less." Caitlyn snagged the pile of lacy boy-cut panties and shooed Calli from the table with a wave of her long, hot-pink fingernails. "I have a hottie lined up for later, don't you worry. What I *don't* have is a pathetic sister. Just one who needs to come with me tonight, so hurry up with all your paperwork. We've got primping to do for our eight o'clock reservation."

Leaving her apartment after dark got easier each time. With Caitlyn's nonstop chatter distracting her, it'd been a piece of cake. The Caitlyn Yates effect.

The restaurant Caitlyn had chosen for their sister-date was in the old factory district by the river. A trendy spot, all of the brown-brick buildings had been converted to shops, restaurants and bars, high-end services. The remodeled facades screamed *pricey*. The packed parking lot told Calli people were okay with that.

"You doing okay?" Caitlyn hooked an arm around Calli's. "You've got that spacey look. Is this too much, too soon?"

"No—no, I'm fine. I was guestimating what the price per square foot might be for one of these units, what the lease terms are and if this area will continue to boom or if the popularity will wane in a couple years."

She didn't laugh, but Caitlyn's smile stretched as wide as physically possible. "You really are fine, aren't you?"

The inky sky with its sparse dotting of stars didn't wrap her in a blanket of terror. Voices from patrons in the parking lot didn't make her jump out of her skin. "I think I am."

"Perfect."

They entered through a set of heavy double doors. Whoever owned The Stacks had done a fantastic job. They'd preserved a lot of the building's character, incorporating some of the old printing-press equipment into the restaurant's theme, both as décor and repurposed pieces. The original high ceilings over the bar and stage areas contrasted with the false beams that'd been added to make the dining sections more intimate and cozy. Lots of metal and concrete fixtures lent to the industrial feel. Rich accent colors, textured fabrics and dropped pendant lighting with colored-glass shades added warmth in all the right places.

"This is incredible."

"Just wait, it gets better," Caitlyn said as they slid into their seats. "First of all, the food is unreal. I had the chicken marsala a couple of nights ago—my mouth had three orgasms."

The too-cute-for-his-own-good host chuckled under his breath, a big mistake around a predator like Caitlyn. She made no bones about checking him out, head to toe. Even licking her super-glossy lips at him before dismissing him by looking the other way.

"He was cute. Kind of had that Mediterranean loverboy vibe you like."

Caitlyn shrugged and flipped through the menu. "I'm not here to pick up."

"Whoa..." For effect, Calli grabbed the table with both hands. "I think the world just tipped on its axis."

"Ooh, my sister the smartmouth is back. You're buying me an eight-dollar martini for that dig."

To think, she'd wanted a way out of this evening. Thank god Caitlyn had bullied her into coming. Calli reached across the table and squeezed her sister's hand. "I'll buy you a *pitcher* of martinis, dinner and dessert. Thank you. For everything."

"I love you, Cal. I'll do any- and everything in my power for you—remember that."

They talked and laughed through dinner. She'd missed so much the past two years. But no more.

The last spoonful of dessert called to her from the edge of the table where she'd pushed it. She ignored it. No room for one more bite in the body-hugging skirt she'd chosen. "Oh my god, I'm stuffed. I bet I consumed ten thousand calories. I may have to cut this skirt off because I doubt I'll get out of it otherwise. But I did have multiple mouth orgasms, so I guess it's a fair trade."

The lighting dimmed and the background music faded. A new smile spread across Caitlyn's face. Satisfied, almost devious.

"The live music is about to start. Maybe you can work off some of those calories later."

If Caitlyn thought she could get Calli onto a dance floor, she'd definitely had one too many Tanqueray martinis. There was taking control of her life, and there was making an ass of herself while attempting to have rhythm. Calli was in for the first one. Full stop.

"I'm not dancing."

"Okay," Caitlyn said.

Hmm. Agreeable enough, but that smile hadn't gone anywhere. What the heck was her sister up t—

"Hey, everybody. Happy Valentine's Day."

Calli's breath caught. No need to turn around, she'd recognize that voice anywhere.

"I'm Travis Graham, and I'll be serenading you diehard romantics tonight." Somebody in the restaurant wolf-whistled. The mic amplified Travis's sexy laugh. "Some of you may not need serenading, by the sounds of it."

Goose bumps rippled over her skin as the first notes from Travis's guitar drifted over the speakers. He was playing. Not pulse-pounding rock with Black Box and not in a huge club, but he was playing.

"He's really good. Better than he was with the band, in my opinion." Caitlyn's words burst the silence at the table. "It was fate that I found him. Or coincidence, take your pick. I was here on a date and voilà, your boyfriend took the stage."

"Coincidence. And ex-boyfriend."

"Semantics."

"He *is* good." The guilt over his injuries wasn't gone, probably never would be, but somewhere inside, the tension she'd been holding on to eased. Now she needed to hold back the tears. "He's why you brought me."

"Well, duh, yeah. It's a nice place, and I love being able to go out to dinner with you again, but when I heard him singing the other night, I knew it was time for you to stop moping and fix things."

"I'm not moping, I've even been dating."

Caitlyn rolled her big blue eyes extra-exaggeratedly. "Puh-leaze, I've seen you get more excited about a cup of hot tea than the guy you're dating."

Fine, so Joe had been gap-filler. That didn't mean Travis hadn't moved on with somebody else—or multiple somebodies—or that he forgave her for ruining his career with Black Box. And it sure didn't mean he wanted her back.

"Did you talk to him—does he know anything?"

"I doubt he even saw me. But does he know that he's in love with you...? Now that's a hell yes, judging by the song he sang the other night."

Hope had no business swelling in her heart. "He sang a song about me... was my name in the lyrics?"

"Listen and find out."

The first two songs were covers. *More Than Words* and *I'm Yours*, both of which pinged her directly in her lovesick heart. Had Travis chosen them because they had meaning to him too, or simply because they were love songs—this being the most romantic day of the year and all. Allegedly, anyway.

The urge to turn around poked at her. Did he still have the facial hair or had he shaved? What was he wearing? He'd told her all about his four guitars, which one was he playing? Was he standing or seated?

When he started singing *Crazy Love*, her willpower disappeared faster than the crème brulée. She had to look. See his face while he sang one of her favorites—a song they'd made love to, their bodies tangled and moving together oh so perfectly.

"Oh god...he's right there," she whispered as she turned. And he was. A couple of tables-for-two stood between her and the man half-sitting on a stool. Fifteen feet, max.

"Yeah, the manager was pretty accommodating when I dropped by to pick out our table."

She would've given Caitlyn the stink-eye, only she couldn't tear her eyes from Travis. He'd only played for her the one time, but shyly—and in hindsight, stupidly—she'd kept her back turned.

Watching him was incredible. So much charisma. He wore his confidence and passion for the music as well as the broken-in jeans and cotton button-up shirt. He'd buzzed most of his hair. Kept the five o'clock shadow. His tattoos made a breathtaking contrast against the white sleeves he'd rolled to his elbows. Honestly, she didn't know which part to focus on—his voice, so deep and rich, his face, with his eyes closed and sinful lips parting as he sang, or his insanely sexy hands moving over the guitar. It was no wonder women threw themselves at him.

It'd been eleven weeks since the break-in. If he had pain in his hand, it didn't show. His movements were fluid. As if the guitar was part of him. With each downward strum, his pinky brushed over what was unmistakably a red rose. *Her* red rose.

She gasped, the slip coming out loud enough to draw attention from the nearby patrons. And from Travis, it seemed. Had he heard her, did he see hers among the faces? His lips curled upward as he launched into the second verse, eyes open this time and focused on her—they had to be.

By the time the song ended, she was holding her

breath. Transfixed, waiting for something that only happened in dreams. She could crash and cry later. Nothing would deprive her of this fantasy moment.

Travis nodded at the applause. "Thank you," he said, laughing when somebody in the back of the restaurant whistled.

The guitar hung from a black leather strap, resting against his body as he tipped a glass of water to his mouth. His Adam's apple slid up and down with each swallow. He emptied the glass, set it on the stool beside him and licked his lips. Good god. The simple act of drinking and the man was sex-on-a-stool.

Warmth spread through Calli's belly, trekking to every cell in her body. When Joe had kissed her, run his hand through her hair, there hadn't been a hint of a spark.

Travis shifted the guitar into position, readying his fingers on the dark neck. All she had to do was look at his hands and her nipples hardened, her clit throbbed. Her body remembered how skillfully those fingers had played *her*. Her chest tightened as he played a few notes of the next song—one she'd only heard the beginning of, three months ago in her kitchen. Her body wasn't the only thing craving Travis. Stupid heart.

"This next song is one of mine," he half-chuckled, "actually, that's not quite right. I wrote it, but it belongs to somebody special." He strummed the first chord. Looked right at her. "So does my heart."

A few people clapped. The guy in the back whistled in approval. Around her, heads turned in her direction. So she wasn't dreaming it—Travis *did* see her.

If that was true... all those beautiful words coming

from his mouth were for her. *About* her. And him. Them.

Calli's heart stuttered. He'd loved her, really? He'd told her that night in the hospital. Not straight-up, but damn close. She'd let it slide, unacknowledged, attributing his words to the trauma of what they'd been through or the drugs they'd pumped into him, or both. But he'd meant them, at the time, at least. Could he still?

The place rocked with applause and hooting when the song ended. Travis smiled. Nodded in appreciation. Kept his eyes on her.

"Go on," Caitlyn poked her from across the table, "what're you waiting for—get up there."

"And do what, hope he doesn't laugh me off the stage?"

"Jeez, Cal, he just serenaded you in front of a hundred people. I know it, he knows it, every other man and woman in here knows it."

Travis refilled his water from a pitcher, still looking at her over the rim while he swallowed it down, one slow sip at a time. Was he waiting for her to make a move? Why didn't he do *something* to let her know?

Caitlyn poked her shoulder again. "Come on, Calli, this is your chance."

Was it? "He didn't ask me to come up or point or anything. He didn't even use my name."

Behind her, Caitlyn groaned. Her chair scraped the tile. Calli forced her eyes from the stage in time to see her sister stand and plant her hands on her hips. Oh shit.

"Hey, Travis," Caitlyn called, drawing every pair of

eyes in the place to where she stood. "Are you in love with my sister?"

Oh god. Calli slid down in her chair. People were staring at her, whispering to each other—about her. And on stage, fifteen feet away, Travis laughed into his mic. Could she shrivel up and die right now, please?

"I think everybody here knows the answer to that," he said. The restaurant could've been a club, the patrons whistled and whooped so loudly. He laughed again, a single deep one. "Yeah, I'm crazy in love with your sister."

More hooting as he stood. He leaned his guitar against the stool. Stepped off the low stage and walked toward her.

With each step closer, Calli's heart hammered harder. If he loved her, why had he dropped out of her life two months earlier, without so much as a goodbye text?

She didn't need to look around to know that she'd become the headlining act. If a single couple remained focused on each other, she'd be amazed. The weight of all those stares made it hard to breathe. Or maybe it was Travis's gaze as he closed the last couple feet between them. Heat flooded her cheeks. Her pulse echoed in her ears. Thank god she was seated, because every inch of her shook.

Instinctively, she accepted his hand, let him bring her to her shaky legs, knowing he'd never let her fall. Not on her ass in this restaurant, not prey to anybody who'd harm her. He was her hero. Her rock-star, Scrabble-playing, hotter-than-hell, real-life romantic hero.

He threaded his fingers through the hair closest to her face. Their descent was slow, purposeful. The restaurant, their audience, disappeared. His fingertips grazed her cheek and she tipped her head, putting her cheek in his palm.

"I've missed you," she said, putting her heart in his hands too. "So much."

"Be my Valentine, sweetheart. Today and every day after."

Most of tables were empty when Travis clicked his guitar case closed. A few late-night couples huddled here and there, oblivious to anybody but their own Valentine's Day date. He knew the feeling—his eyes hadn't left Calli more than five minutes the entire evening. Once he'd gotten his hands on her, literally, he'd determined not to let her get away again. Not ever, if he had the option. Not until they'd had a chance to talk, if nothing else.

He'd snagged an empty chair and deposited her in front of the stage. Ninety minutes later, that's where she remained, those big, beautiful eyes following him as he packed up. She'd missed him? He paused for another long look at his buttoned-up siren, grinning when her pretty face turned pink. If she let him, he planned to show her exactly how much he'd missed her.

"Want to wait inside while I bring my car to the door?" He still didn't know how she'd done it—gotten here, beaten the fear. He'd seen firsthand what happened when she went outside after dark. Yet she'd gone to the hospital after the attack. Now this—out at night in a busy restaurant, strictly for fun and looking sexy as hell.

"Not unless you're parked six blocks away, in which case, yes, because these shoes are more the standing-around-looking-stylish kind, as opposed to the easy-to-walk-in type."

His eyes traveled over her shapely calves to the spiky heels. Mile-high strappy purple things he couldn't imagine having to take two steps in, though he was in no hurry for her to take them off. Unless her preference for garters and stockings had changed, she wouldn't have to.

He shifted his eager cock, not all that discreetly, if Calli's smile was indication. Didn't bother him. Let her see how she affected him simply by sitting there. Fair warning for the rest of the night. He collected his stuff, then his woman, pulling her up from the chair.

She glanced at their joined hands. "Does it hurt?"

"Not right now." He squeezed as proof. "Is this your way of telling me that I played like shit tonight?" Cool air greeted them when they left the restaurant behind and stepped out into the night. In the dark and she was still okay. Glowing, even. So incredibly beautiful.

"God no. You were amazing...I had no idea. I mean, I knew you must be good, but..." Her hand slid free of his and wrapped around his waist before delving lower to fondle his butt. The eyes focused on his were filled with naughty. "You officially have a new number-one fan. And like a good groupie, I plan to do whatever it takes to seduce you, Mr. Graham."

The clicking of her heels on the asphalt stopped as they reached his car. He set his guitar aside. Caged her against the cold door with his arms. "No need for formality, sweetheart. Call me Travis."

"Okay... Travis."

He groaned and leaned into her. Too many days and lonely nights had gone by without hearing her say his name. Those wicked high heels added about four inches to her height, but he still had to dip his head to kiss her luscious lips. Warm and sweet, they parted for him. He stroked into her mouth, her tongue meeting his and urging it deeper.

The clink of metal echoed in the near-vacant lot. Between them, she'd deftly unbuckled his belt, opened his button and lowered his zipper. She fished him free of his boxers. Curled her soft fingers around his aching cock and slid her fist up and down with deliberate, torturous slowness. Fucking hell, another minute of this and he'd be done for.

"Let me take you home, make you come all night long."

"After," she said, then went to her knees and sucked him into her mouth, right there in the middle of the parking lot.

"You don't have to do this here..." He breathed another curse as she tongued pre-cum from the tip. "We can get in the car first." She giggled around his cock. He let his head fall back and thanked the heavens above that she didn't take him up on the offer.

His breath made clouds against the crisp night air. He looked down at the dark-haired goddess making love to his cock with her lips and hands. Sucking and licking him as if she'd been starved for him. Her eyes fluttered open and met his—practically silver in the moonlight. He lifted his right hand from the car, ran it through her hair.

"Mmm-hmm," vibrated around his cock. Again when he wrapped a section of silky strands around his fist.

Hell, he felt her smile as much as he saw it. Staring up at him—*into him*—with wide eyes, she let him pop free of her lips. Her tongue darted out to tease his steadily leaking slit.

"This is one of my favorite parts." She licked the drops, sucked him between her lips nice and hard, then returned to orally caressing his cock head between words. "But I love it when you're deep in my throat too. When you're past the point of no return, throbbing in my mouth. Feed me your cock, Travis. Let me take you over the edge."

"Anything to make you happy." He smiled and pushed into her mouth, slowly, savoring the soft, warm suction as she welcomed every inch. If he closed his eyes, thought about something else, he could hold out longer. Another time. Right now he didn't want to blink. Didn't want to miss a fraction of a second.

She nodded, nostrils flaring when he cupped her head and brought her closer. She sucked him greedily, her tongue swirling around his cock while her fingernails dug into his ass.

"Fuck, too good, too good..." he bit out as his knees buckled, his cock pulsing in satisfaction. He slumped over her. Stroked her hair. Shuddered when she released him with a final lick. "Come up here." He helped her to her feet, brushed his fingers up the delicate column of her neck and cupped her face between his hands. "All the times I dreamed we'd be together again, a blowjob outside, in the dark, was never the way."

"Are you disappointed that I went groupie on you out

here in the cold instead of waiting until we got to a safe, warm bed?"

"Disappointed that the woman I love is the hottest, sexiest groupie in the world—not a fucking chance."

"Good. Now take me home and make me come all night long."

Chapter Twelve

If he'd given in to Calli back at her apartment, they'd be naked right now. Kissing at minimum, probably a hell of a lot more. Not... this.

"See, staying at my place would've been easier and less, um, hair-raising."

Another tumbleweed of black cat fur rolled to his feet as Calli's Chihuahua and his once-fluffy cat completed circuit two hundred fifty-four around his small open-concept apartment.

"No, this is good. We're going to be together, so they're going to be together." He wrapped his arms around Calli's waist and pulled her ass snug to his groin. "And it looks like Kersh is finally getting tired. Or maybe he's hungry from burning off two days' worth of kibble. Either way, I think he's going to give PC a break in ten laps or less."

The top of Calli's head pressed into his chest as she tipped her face up. "PC?"

"If anybody's going to be your Prince Charming, it's going to be me." He yanked them both backward to avoid a head-to-leg collision with one of the tan and black streaks. "Plus, PC and I had a man-to-dog chat while you were packing a bag. He said Charming was cute when he was an indoor dog, but now that he's a dog on the street, it's a little embarrassing."

"My dog told you he prefers PC to Charming?"

"That he did."

"Uh-huh."

God, she was cute when she got that saucy look. He spun her to face him. "You think I'm making this up?"

"Yes, Mr. Hot Rock Star Stud, I think you're full of shit."

"Care to wager that I'm not, Ms. Secret Sex Kitten?"

She wiggled closer, eyes widening at the hard mass pressing against her belly. "You love playing games, don't you?"

"When they get you out of your clothes, yes."

"No need to bet to make that happen."

He stopped her hand on the top button. "Whoa. Out of your clothes the way I tell you to, sweetheart. I want you to strip while you dance for me. You've owed me an erotic dance since our first Scrabble game."

"I don't dance, I've told you that."

"If you're right about your dog, you won't have to worry about it." Much as he hated to put space between them, he walked to one end of the room, motioning her to go to the other. "On three, we'll call him." Ballsy move, now he just hoped it'd work.

"One, two, three—" Both names filled the room. The Chihuahua hit the brakes mid-loop, looked from Travis to Calli, even gave his feline nemesis a glance. For a split-second, it could've gone either way. Then, victory.

"Oh my god, I can't believe he chose you. What a little traitor."

Neither could he. He'd still take it. "This way to my bedroom, sweetheart. Bring your best moves." He grabbed his acoustic and bit the inside of his cheek. Hard not to grin when she had her arms crossed and her bottom lip sticking out.

"How long have you lived here?" She set her bag on the floor while doing a quick scan of the room.

"Two years."

"Oh." Her eyes swept over the bare white walls. Took in his low bed with its plain navy duvet, the boxy dresser, an assemble-it-yourself special. "My bedroom must drive you nuts, all the colors and pillows and… stuff."

"Not at all. I never bothered to do anything with this place because it didn't matter. All I do here is—"

Calli waved her hands in front of her face. "Stop."

"Is sleep. Alone. Well, other than Kersh." He dropped the guitar on the bed. Grabbed her by the waist and tugged her close. Too much tension in her body—because of him. His past, their history, his mistakes with both. "I've never brought a woman here. You're the first," he nudged her hair aside to kiss her neck, "and the last."

"Why, are you planning on moving?"

Funny girl. "Yeah, somewhere with a yard for our dog."

"What—you—*our* dog?"

God, she was adorable when she sputtered. "Not tonight. But if I don't make you crazy—"

"Crazier, you mean."

Is that really how she saw herself, still? He pulled her onto the bed with him, on their sides and face-to-face. "You're not crazy. Never were."

"We both know I was. But I'm getting better."

"Getting? You beat it." He put a finger to her lips before she could jump in. "Don't even try giving credit to the pills you told me about, or the therapy or anything else. It was all you walking out of the restaurant tonight. Head up and no hesitation. Beautiful."

She pushed his finger away with a kiss. "Thank you."

A bit of tugging and he managed to get her rubber-band of a skirt high enough to palm the satiny skin of her ass. It'd been way too long since he'd had his hands on her body. Having his cock in her mouth an hour ago was fantastic, but not nearly enough. The fifty times he'd kissed her since then weren't enough, either.

He wedged his quadriceps between her thighs. Pulled her close as he could get her and tasted the lips that'd made him see stars on a starless night.

"Yeah, you certainly weren't afraid of the dark in the parking lot."

She giggled and cupped a hand over his bulging fly. "So you like the new me."

"I loved the old you, Calli. Whether you're inside or out, I'm crazy about you."

Her lips parted as if to answer, only to close again. His gut, his heart, her incredible eyes—all told him she felt the same. Not that he deserved her after the dick he'd been. Fate had stepped in, allowed him to save her from a psycho. A huge stroke of luck and coincidence had landed him this third chance with her. No fucking it up this time.

"I'm still in shock about that son-of-a-bitch, Barros. I should've killed him, wish I had."

"I get chills thinking about it...what would've happened if you hadn't been online that night, if I hadn't given in to my moment of weakness and invited you to play, if you hadn't accepted..." Hair fell over her face as she trembled in his arms.

He tucked it behind her shoulder, letting his hand linger in its softness. "Barros wouldn't have had a chance to get near you if I hadn't screwed up in the first place. I would've been there to protect you."

"Not every night. Not the nights you went on the road." She twisted out of his arms and off the bed. "If it weren't for me, you'd be onstage at some huge club right now, or in a studio recording tracks for the album deal Black Box just signed."

"You know about that?"

"Of course I know. I cyber-stalked you after we broke up. Both times. It's a girl thing."

"I think it's an *us* thing." Wrong time to smile, but he

couldn't help it. They were quite a pair. Had been from their first meeting online.

"They took your name off the website right after the attack. I kept checking for it to go back up, but it never did. After all the work you did for that band, onstage and behind the scenes, those bastards replaced you the second you got hurt—because of *me*."

Charging to his defense—he really didn't deserve her. "It wasn't as bad as you think."

"Don't be nice. I cost you a huge opportunity, your music career." She'd yanked the skirt back in place, buttoned the top button. Now she was working on buttons that didn't need fastening, just to avoid looking at him. "I don't blame you for walking away after that night in the hospital... "

What the hell? "You did the walking, sweetheart. Out of my room, out of my life. A couple of impersonal texts to check on my injuries, then that last one where you very politely let me know you were moving on." Somehow he'd gone from lying on his bed with the woman he'd been missing for months to standing in front of her with smoke coming out his ears. "But after what I did that night in the club, then the way I took advantage of you in the hospital, I didn't blame *you* for not looking back."

Her eyes snapped from the floor to his face. "I forgave what you *almost* did in that bar. On the spot. You didn't accept it."

"You're right. I wasn't ready to be forgiven."

"I tried to hate you for it. Came close for a couple of days. I even decided you were right—about me deserving better. I did. I do."

"Good." He deserved every word. Hated them, but deserved them.

She reached for his shirt, hesitated. Looked at him through those long eyelashes and the thick bangs dusting her eyebrows, then slid her fingers between the buttons. "You know how difficult it is to have a serious conversation with you when I can see your sexy tattoos through this thin white shirt?"

What the...? Calli ought to come with warning labels, the woman could change direction so fast. Not that he minded in this case. She'd taken him from hot under the collar to hot all over with a fingertip touch, a look and a comment. Half a dozen buttons later, the shirt was on the floor at her feet. Maybe he flexed a little too.

"There. Now you can get back to being serious." And damn it, she'd better hurry up. The flush on her face and shine in her eyes was getting to him, fast. With every flick of her tongue over her lips, he got ten seconds closer to telling her they'd talk later. Much later.

"I, uh... can you stop popping your pecs for thirty seconds and let me focus?"

Busted. "Want me to turn around?"

"As if that'll help. Your back is as hot as your front." Her eyes dropped to his low-slung jeans. "Well, almost." A little shake of her head and her eyes returned to his face. "God, I can't even remember what I was talking about."

This had to be the best make-up fight in the history of making up. "About my mistakes. The way I blew it by taking advantage of you in the hospital, pushing things too fast."

The cutest indignant snort popped from her mouth.

"You did *not* take advantage of me in the hospital. I'm the one who sexually abused a seriously injured man, blew out his stitches while riding him to oblivion—"

"We're talking about me, right?"

"*Travis.*"

"Watch it with the name calling, or we won't get through this serious part before I tear those buttons open and get started on the making-you-come-all-night part."

She rolled her eyes and laughed, and it was the sweetest sound in the world. "Can I finish?"

"Many times, that's my plan."

"You're so bad."

He caught the hand she poked him with and held it over his heart. "But I'm trying to be better. I stand by what I said that night—you deserve a good man. I want to be him."

"Then don't change a thing."

And they were back at serious. "I fought those damn painkillers as long as I could after they sewed me up again, but you didn't come back. I passed out. Slept for hours. And when I asked about you in the morning, you'd gone. No goodbye, nothing."

"I couldn't. I knew once it sank in about your hand, you'd resent me. Maybe worse."

"You didn't give me a chance. Not to be angry, not tell you that I wasn't."

"I texted you. Aside from answering my questions, you didn't say... anything."

"Like that I was in love with you?" He grabbed her by the hips. Yanked her to him. "Oh, wait, I did that. In person, in the hospital. You ignored it."

"You were loopy on drugs, it didn't count."

"Unless they pumped me full of Viagra, it was pretty obvious I was in control of myself."

Her mouth ticked up the tiniest bit at his last statement. Maybe at the memory—he hoped. Then it was gone.

"I cost you so much... why would you want to be with me?"

"Sweetheart, you *gave* me so much. I was so sick of being that guy, I hated myself, hated everybody around me because all they wanted from me was a party guy from a rock band. I left Black Box, not the other way around. I'd wanted to quit for months, but I didn't have the balls to do it, to go out on my own. The songs I played tonight, the ones I wrote—that's the music I want to make. You're my muse, Calli. For my music, for me, as a man. Everything's better since I met you. Even if you don't want me—and I sure as hell don't deserve you to—I'm not going back."

There was barely an inch between them. Could've been a canyon. Her eyes traveled his face, slowly taking in every line and piece of stubble. Could she see the truth, how much she meant to him?

"You were afraid of the dark too."

He had to laugh. "I pour my heart out in that eloquent speech and you sum it up in one sentence."

"I have a way with words, what can I say? I'll let you

use it for a song, as long as I'm in the credits."

If any other woman had suggested, even jokingly, that he write a song—hell, sing a song—for her, he'd have sneered, then run in the opposite direction. Those days were done. He sat on the corner of the mattress and dragged his Taylor acoustic onto his lap.

"Let's try it out. See how it feels." He scrubbed his hand along his jaw while searching his mind for a starting note. Shit, his face felt like sixty-grit sandpaper. If he'd half a clue he'd be near Calli, he'd have lost the scruff. "I'll shave this."

"Don't you dare—not until I try *it* out to see how it feels. Against my nipples... and my thighs." With shaky hands, she popped the top button of her blouse. Travis had laid himself out there for her—her turn next. "Play something. I can't give you that dance I owe you without music."

With his dark hair, soft hazel eyes, sort-of-dangerous five o'clock shadow and those ridiculously sexy tattoos covering two-thirds of his upper body, Travis was already a ten on the hottie scale. But when he smiled—that genuine, soul-deep smile that seemed to light him up from the inside out—he became completely irresistible. She'd do anything for him... including her first-ever striptease.

He started to play. Nothing familiar, but whatever song it was, it was perfect for the job.

She'd danced plenty of times. Only in front of her dog, but hey, he hadn't turned tail and run. And Travis had seen her move—very intimately, every which way and fully naked. If she could do those things while looking into his eyes, a little bump and grind while she took her clothes off was nothing. She could do this.

She closed her eyes and let Travis's music flood her senses. The sultry beat worked its way through her body. She let her hips swivel side to side, then into a figure-eight. She relaxed her neck, rolled her shoulders, matching the rhythm of her hips. The music took over, guiding her as she made a slow half turn, bent at the waist and arched her back.

Behind her, he groaned. The sound of pure masculine hunger shot to her core, empowering her. She ran her hands downward over her ass as she swayed. She curled her fingers under the hem and eased the skirt up, one slow inch at a time, until it bunched around her waist, leaving her bare except for the strip of purple lace masquerading as underwear and the matching garters stretching over her ass to the tops of her stockings.

"God damn."

The huskiness in his voice unlocked something inside her. She turned again, managing to unzip and step out of the god-forsakenly tight skirt in the process without falling on her face—no small miracle with her eyes closed and the mile-high spiky heels she still wore. She brought her hands up, twining them together above her head before letting them fall to the row of silver buttons on her sheer black blouse.

"I want to see your eyes."

Her eyelids fluttered open and she met his gaze. Intense, hungry, appreciative. "Better?" she whispered around her heart, now stuck in her throat.

"Perfect."

"Oh?" She ran her index finger up and down over the

buttons. "Then I should leave these closed?"

"If you don't open them, you know I will."

By popping them off in one swoop as he'd done before, she bet. Very hot, but she'd prefer to wear this blouse again. "Keep your hands off my buttons," she said, working the second one through its hole.

"No deal."

"Okay, don't." She pushed the last silver disc clear of the fabric. Goose bumps rose on her arms as the material slid over her skin. The bra followed suit, tickling her nipples to hard peaks. She cupped her naked breasts. Kneaded them. Pushed them together while his eyes burned into her. "Touch all my buttons. These ones…" She thumbed the straining, needy nipples, then trailed her fingers lower, into the front of her tiny thong. "This one."

The music ended mid-strum. He shoved the guitar aside, shucked his jeans and boxer-briefs in one movement and crooked a finger at her. A tractor beam couldn't have been more effective. She glided forward, into the vee between his legs.

He stopped her hand when she pulled it from her panties. "Keep it there."

Obediently, she snaked her hand beneath the satin again. Her clit was slippery under her fingers. Desperate for pressure. She rubbed it, a small circle to relieve the aching need for contact, and couldn't stifle the moan of pleasure. Her cheeks burned at the noisy slip, but when she braved meeting Travis's eyes, she'd never seen them so dark.

"Do that again," he said, then closed his mouth over

one nipple.

Soft warmth washed over her first. Gentle, sensual laving. Then teeth, scraping her sensitive areola, nipping the tip of her stiff peak. Delicious roughness from his stubble as it brushed her skin. Pleasure as she'd only experienced with one man—Travis.

She moaned louder, pressed her fingers harder against her clit. Her knees buckled—stupid pretty shoes—and she stumbled forward, toppling them onto the bed in a tangle of limbs, lips and laughter.

Both animals tore into the room. Shoulder to shoulder, they surveyed the state of their humans. Satisfied with what he saw, Charming nosed Kersh, wagged his tail, and the chase was on again.

"I think they're playing now, not fighting."

"Like us." Travis ran his fingertips under the string on her hip, pure mischief glinting in his eyes. "How much do you like these?"

"I hate them."

His grin was feral. His arm flexed and the scrap of material fell away from her body.

"Good thing I have access to an unlimited supply of panties."

"I wouldn't mind if you went without. Easier access for me to do this..." He trailed his fingers over her heated core, torturing her with a light touch to her clit, then hinting at penetration only to remove his hand at the last second. "Or this..." He rolled her onto her back and hauled her knees over his shoulders. Head caged by her thighs, he dipped into her—lips and tongue, teeth and fingers.

Bliss, simple as that. "God, I've missed this. No toys compare to your—everything."

His mouth vibrated against her, might've been a laugh, maybe a growl. Either way, the sensation ratcheted up her need.

She cupped his head, the buzzed hair soft under her palms as she gave into the spiral beginning between her legs. Her hips thrust upward, eager for more delicious pressure, more of his fingers curling inside her while he sucked and flicked her clit. Over she flew. She clutched at him, bucking through a climax that left her breathless. And ready for more.

She waited for him to look up and meet her eyes. "I'm all yours."

Six feet of gorgeous, naked, very hard man rose to stand in front of her. Too yummy to simply look at. She rolled onto hands and knees and crawled across the bed toward him.

He stopped her with a small head shake and a smile. "You have no idea what it does to me, watching you stare at my cock and lick your lips. Makes me want to—"

"To what?" she asked, positioning herself at exactly the right height for him to slide over her bottom lip, deep into her mouth.

Only he didn't. "Not this time."

"But I love sucking you. It makes me hot."

"You're already hot."

She darted a lick at the tip before he had a chance to

step away. "It makes me wet."

A single laugh burst from his lips. "You're already wet. You were wet before my tongue touched you." He chuckled again, dropping to his haunches and catching her chin in his hand when she pouted. "Sweetheart, I didn't think I'd ever see you again, let alone have you in my bed and in my life. I need to be inside you. Deep inside you, right now."

"I can't really argue with that."

"Good." His lips brushed hers lightly. "Now turn around so I can fuck you."

She couldn't argue with that, either. A drawer opened and closed as she changed position. Foil ripped. She looked over her shoulder in time to see him roll a condom over his thick, rigid cock. Honestly, the man was spectacular. She may never use her Mr. Right Magnum Eight again. Unless...

"Travis..." She hadn't meant to whisper, but her heart was racing, stealing her ability to breathe deeply or speak any louder. "Can you grab my bag?"

One dark eyebrow rose. Three seconds later the canvas tote dropped on the bed.

"Open it. Take your pick, use anything you want." They'd had nothing but phenomenal sex, loaded with dirty talk that included telling each other various things they wanted to do. They just hadn't had the time to do them all before the break-up. Now they did.

Travis's eyes left her to peruse the contents of her hastily packed bag. A smile quirked at his mouth, pulled the corners of his eyes into creases. "You have quite a selection here."

From the temperature of her face, she had to be past pink and approaching red. So what—he liked it when she blushed. She wiggled her hips to draw his attention. Once she had his gaze, she ran a hand over her backside, dipped her fingertips in her juices and dragged them upward until she got to the rim of her ass. Slowly, she circled, teasing herself as much as him.

"See anything that interests you?"

The bed dipped as he moved to his knees behind her. "Everything. But right now, this." He trapped her hand with his. Put gentle pressure on her middle finger—the teasing one—enough to breach the tight ring of muscle and nerves. Another press from his hand urged her finger deeper. "Fuck, Calli. Just...fuck." He exhaled, long, low and appreciatively. "How does it feel?"

"Good." Her eyes were on his face, but his were focused on her ass, their joined hands. God, he was gorgeous. Sexy. Inextinguishably hot. "But—" Now his eyes flicked to her face. Perfect. "It's not enough...I want more, I want to be filled."

A pained groan came from her man. "You're killing me."

"Get the blue vibrator with the rhinestones around the base." She almost giggled at the speed with which he rifled through the bag. "That's the one. It turns on by twisting the base. The more you turn it, the more—"

"It vibrates." He closed his palm around the smooth cylinder, clearly assessing its power and girth. "And this is for..."

"It's an anal toy."

His Adam's apple slid up and down and he licked his lips. "Is it new?" His normally rich voice had become a low rasp.

What answer was he hoping for? She shook her head, smiled a little. "No, I've used it. A few times."

"Tell me how." The head of his cock bumped against her, sliding inside her instantly, making them both groan at the promise of what was to come—literally. "Every detail." Hands braced on her back, including the one holding the vibrator, he prevented her from pushing onto his cock, engulfing him like she wanted. "Ah-ah. Not until you tell me."

"Meanie."

"You started it, sweetheart."

She swiveled her hips a little and another groan escaped his lips. Two could play the meanie-pants teaser game. "Sometimes I lie on my back and fuck myself in the ass with it while I rub my clit."

"Sweet Jesus." An inch, maybe two, of his cock slid forward. One-handed, he twisted the jeweled base. Tickled her with the softly whirring toy. He used some of the wetness from between her legs to lubricate his target, then pressed the sloping tip against her. "You come with this in your ass?"

"Mmm-hmm." She squirmed against it, trying to get more, but he didn't give it to her. God, what was he waiting for?

"More," he said between gritted teeth.

"Yes please."

He laughed. A short, sexy bark that shot an arrow straight into her heart. Right then, she knew. No more talking herself out of it—she loved him. She'd give him anything he wanted, with pleasure.

"One time, I was on my stomach. I waited until I was almost coming, then slid it all the way in and—" The swift thrust of his cock stole her breath and her words. She fumbled around with one arm until she hit the bag. Found the lube and lobbed it in his general direction.

A cool trickle slid down her backside. "Like this?" he asked, inching the vibe deeper.

"Yes... keep going... give me more... all of it."

"Oh fuck." Travis pulled out, thrust his cock deep inside her again, mimicking the movement with the toy in her ass.

Sensations bombarded her. The pounding of his cock, the fluttering inside as he ratcheted the vibrator higher. Skin smacking against skin with each hard, perfect thrust. So good.

"I want more," she said, practically gasping the words.

"That's all of it, sweetheart—it and me—I feel like I've got a fucking cannon down there, you're turning me on so much."

"Mmm, I feel it, I love it." She scraped her nails across her ass cheeks, pulling them apart ever-so-slightly while she met his eyes. "I want that cannon in my ass."

"You're sure?"

"You really have to ask?"

He chuckled at her whimper when he removed the

toy. "Fuck, you're sexy." The tip of his cock nudged her rear. He let out a strangled moan as the head eased inside. "I'll go slow, I promise."

She didn't want slow. Her lips parted to tell him, but all that came out was this... sound. Something new, low and primal, it matched what she wanted. What she needed.

"More." She pushed her hips backward. A demand. "All."

"Fuck." He groaned and slid deeper. Deeper. "Fuuuck... I have to—" He pulled back, thrust into her again. "Fuck, so good." Retreated and thrust, harder. "Can't stop—fuck, Calli, you're so—fucking—tight—perfect—fuck..."

God, the fullness. She moaned every time he slid home. Almost cried out. It bordered on pain, so fiery hot and intense, yet she craved it. Whimpered with each retreat. Arched her hips to welcome each new thrust.

"Deeper..." Her skin tingled. Between her legs, she ached with the need to come.

Travis's hand on her back guided her lower, to her stomach. He stretched her legs flat and straight, between his. Then moved inside her again.

"Oh god... oh..." The angle, the position—whatever it was, just... did it. Tipped the scale, tilted the whole world. She jammed both hands under her body. Curled her fingers around her clit. Ground her body against her knuckles, setting off an explosion that rippled along every inch of skin cradling his pumping cock.

Travis yelled a string of curses and collapsed on her back, forcing the air from her lungs. "Shit, sorry, I'm crushing you."

Her hands scrambled to cup his ass. "It's perfect, don't move." And it was. The weight of him, the heat. Comfort, protection and passion in one. Their skin, slick with sweat and the scent of sex. More than that. "I love you."

He shifted enough to brush her hair aside, then pressed a tender kiss below her ear. "Forever, sweetheart. This time, it's forever."

Epilogue

Calli took the back stairs two at a time. The store was a mess and she hadn't done the daily paperwork—it'd be there later. She'd never complain about paying customers, especially when the last couple had dropped close to five hundred bucks *and* bought three pieces of her handmade jewelry, but they'd come in ten minutes before closing and now she was late for her date. Hopefully he'd waited.

"Shit," she said to Charming by way of greeting. "I don't suppose you'd use your pan for old times' sake?" The eyes bugging out of his face at her said no, and not in nice terms. "Okay, but it's going to be a quick one."

Six o'clock on a beautiful July evening. The sun was still high and a warm breeze wafted the aroma of a street vendor's cart somewhere in the neighborhood. Her stomach rumbled harder as her dog demanded they follow the scent half a block down Belmont.

In the end she had to pick up the stubborn Chihuahua and carry him home. He wasn't particularly impressed at the mode of transport. Neither was she. Now she was thirty-five minutes behind schedule.

Inside the apartment, she grabbed her laptop and headed for the bedroom. Two sets of legs followed.

"Ugh, I'm hungry too, but since *I'm* waiting, you guys can wait."

Two pairs of eyes stared up from the floor. Charming and Kersh didn't give a hoot about her online date. They wanted kibble, stat.

"Fine." She logged in, raced to the kitchen to feed the boys and returned to the computer in a matter of minutes. "Be there, be there, don't let it be too late..."

She simultaneously sighed and smiled. The animated host waved at her, holding a card that read, *Travis has invited you to play. Accept this player or decline?*

She clicked the button and the screen switched to a game board. Didn't matter how many times they'd played, her heart still jumped when she saw Travis's avatar. He'd ditched the black rose shortly after Valentine's Day, swapping it for a photo of Kersh spooning Charming. Of all the things he could've used for his avatar, he'd chosen a picture of "the kids", as he called it. If it was possible to love him more, she didn't know how.

He'd played *waiting* for eighty points. Double-letter score on the W, double-word score and a damn bingo—a fifty-point bonus for playing all seven tiles in one shot. He must have an in with the admins now that he'd done some revamp work on the Wordloverz site, because he always seemed to have the perfect tiles at exactly the right time.

The best word she could come up with was *dong* for eight measly points. At least it was appropriate.

Not surprisingly, he commented. **Nice word.**

She pictured him smiling at his screen, shaking his head in amusement. **Sold a big one right before closing time.**

As big as the one in the back of your t-shirt drawer?

The rat. How'd he know about her secret stash, the

goodies she kept for use while he was traveling? All *their* toys were in the night table.

Another message popped up on his side of the chat window. ***Have you used it this week? How about the little black one you like so much?***

The only black item she owned was a thumb-sized vibrator she'd felt obligated to test drive before shelving at Romance U, since it retailed at ninety-nine dollars.

He'd questioned her about the price while adding it to the online store, and she'd assured him it was worth the money. He'd poked and teased at her until she confessed to sampling one enough to wear down its first charge. Travis being Travis, he'd immediately checked the specs in the info he was uploading to see how long the little unit claimed to last. To say he'd been jealous of the toy's time between her legs was kind of an understatement.

She rolled across the bed. Travis was spontaneous, but never random. He'd asked her about a specific item— there had to be a reason. He'd probably taken it—maybe everything—with him, just for fun. She'd been so busy this week, she'd nodded off every night without opening the drawer once.

She pulled the handle, wondering what she would or wouldn't find. The Black Magic sat in its velvet-lined box, a sticky note wrapped around the end of its shiny shaft. She peeled the yellow paper away, smoothed it on the tabletop, smiling as her fingers traced the indent of his pencil-scrawled words. *I can do better than this. XO.*

Tears welled in the corners of her eyes. He'd been gone six days this time, and she'd done a decent job of keeping occupied so she wasn't constantly pining. It was only going to get worse—the nights away to play out of town had turned into weekend gigs, sometimes three- or four-day stints with travel time.

This trip was much bigger than those. A music exec had scouted him at a club and invited him to record a three-song demo at a schmanzy Toronto studio, all expenses paid. The opportunity of a lifetime. If it went well, he could end up signed to a label, have singles on the radio, music videos, on tour...

The laptop beeped as a new message appeared. **Still there? It's your move, sweetheart.**

She shook her head, focused on the screen. He'd played *love* for seven points. That promise she'd made to herself not to be a whiny, needy girlfriend crumbled.

I wish you were here.

Black vibrator run out of charge again?

Smartass. **Haven't touched it. Waiting for somebody who does it better.** There, now he knew she'd seen his note.

That's a lucky somebody. Do I know him?

A smile replaced the tears that'd threatened. **He has brown hair, hazel eyes, a giant, hairy mole on his stomach and a third arm growing out of his side. Oh, and he carries a Scrabble board. Always.**

Sounds dangerously nerdy.

Mmm-hmm. Actually, he's deliciously nerdy. If he were here right now, I'd drop to my knees and suck his cock until he yelled bingo.

Seconds ticked into minutes without a reply. Or a move. Probably meant he'd had to answer a call or a text.

Flirting online with your girlfriend obviously took a backseat to more important business. She got it, she did. And she couldn't be more happy and proud of him, but damn it, sometimes it really sucked.

Berserk yipping and scurrying sounds startled her from her funk. Her heart had jumped out of her chest with the surprise, but she wasn't scared. She'd been off the Alprazolam for three full months, and the fearful part of her was still gone. It was moments like this that reminded her of that victory, made her smile head-to-toe.

The frenzied barking notched down to excited whining. In her haste to get online, she hadn't pulled the living room blinds. With everything going on in the Village this weekend, Charming was bound to go bananas at the low-slung windows.

She hopped off the bed, putting on her authoritative voice as she stepped into the hall. "Charming. Kersh is going to be mad at you when I have to shut out the sunshine..."

"That's what I told him."

"Oh my god!" She squealed at the sight of Travis standing in the middle of the room. "You weren't supposed to be back until Monday..." She flung herself at him, only giving up squeezing him when the possibilities barged into her head. "Why *are* you home early, did something go wrong in the studio, or in the meetings?" Because as much as she'd love to have him around 24/7, she'd love seeing his dream come true more.

"Hey, watch the Scrabble board tucked under my arm here..." He winked and set his netbook on the coffee table.

"Huh?"

"Not the real deal, I know, but the best I could do on five minutes' notice. I was parked in front of the coffee shop, taking advantage of their free WiFi while I waited for the right opportunity to surprise you. Didn't want to drive around the city looking for another Scrabble board when I had such a great offer waiting for me upstairs."

"Offer? Oh, *that* offer." She went to her knees, more than happily, and unzipped his jeans. His half-ready cock swelled in her grip. One swipe of her tongue around the head and he stopped her, pulling her to her feet.

"You've got it backward, sweetheart." This time *he* lowered—to one knee. He pulled a box from his pocket and cracked it open, offering up an amazing smile and the most beautiful amethyst-and-diamond ring she'd ever seen. "Say you'll be mine."

"I'm yours," she blurted.

"If you wouldn't mind clarifying, there are three males in the room, and I'm pretty sure all of us would like that distinction."

He didn't fool her. For whatever reason, he loved when she said his name. She'd hated her voice since the first attack damaged her throat, stripping away the higher pitch forever. Knowing that Travis found her husky tone sexy, that hearing her speak his name turned him on, had gotten her past that resentment. Meeting him, falling in love with him, had been the catalyst that changed everything. She'd been his since day one—he had to know that.

"I'm yours, Travis." Her voice shook. Her knees were worse. He steadied her. Slid the ring on the *index* finger of her left hand...

He laughed, gut deep and all the way to his eyes. "You are so damn cute when you scrunch your eyebrows together like that." His thumb rubbed soft circles over her hand. "I'm asking you for forever, yes, but I figured I'd keep the traditional finger open until I can afford to get you a big diamond for it—which won't be too far down the road, since I signed a contract this afternoon."

"Oh my god, I'm so, so happy for you!"

"Will you keep that spot open for me, Calli—marry me when I'm in a position to give you everything you deserve?"

His hair was longer again, thick and soft under her fingers. "You don't have to do this now. I don't expect you to stay in every night playing Scrabble when you're going to have the world at your feet. It's a beautiful ring, and a wonderful promise," she screwed the white-gold band off her finger and held it out, "but you should keep them both, at least for a while."

"You think I gave you a ring out of some twisted sense of obligation?" The smile vanished, replaced by a hard line. "I got it the week after we got back together. I've almost given it to you a hundred times, but I wanted to have more to offer you than part-time work building websites and intermittent gigs that might never amount to more." On his feet now, he stared down at her. "When're you going to believe me that—"

"I love you." She didn't say it enough. She didn't believe it enough when Travis said it. "I got you something too. Wait for me for a minute?"

"Forever."

"It won't take that long." Thank god for the crinkles around his eyes, the slight twitch of his lips. She hurried to their bedroom, hands shaking as she undressed. Too many buttons and hooks. One of these days she'd start wearing t-shirts and yoga pants, to speed the process along.

She pulled a new black-lace bra and skimpy boyshorts from her drawer. Fastened the thin leather choker she'd made around her neck. Stepped into ridiculously high fuck-me shoes. She did a quick perusal in the mirror, running a finger over the design disappearing into the top of her panties. If he hated it... well, there was always laser removal. She took a deep breath and returned to the living room.

"Holy fucking hell. I should stay away more often."

"As long as you always come home to me."

"Only place I want to be, sweetheart." He closed the gap between them and put his hands on her. In her hair, down the valley of her breasts, under the collar around her neck, around the ink wrapping her hip. "You got a tattoo."

"I went to your guy—he was really good, like you said."

"Jamie's one of the best."

A glowing rec for the tattoo artist, not for the permanent addition to her body. Crap. "You hate it."

His eyes flicked from the ink to her eyes. "No, hell no. Just surprised, you've never mentioned getting one. It looks incredible on you. The dark lines and hints of color against your fair skin are perfect."

So he hadn't noticed yet. "Look closer."

"With pleasure. Mind if I start at the top and work my way down?" It wasn't a question so much as a warning. Travis placed a light kiss on her forehead, each eyelid, the tip of her nose. His lips met hers, softly at first. Gentle but not hesitant. A slow, sensual tease as he increased the pressure, exploring her mouth in a way that made her squeeze her thighs together to ease the budding need. Travis was always in control—he knew what he wanted, what she wanted too—and always made both happen, to her never-ending delight.

The next stop was her neck. He licked and nipped his way down the side, chuckling when she shivered.

"This is pretty," he said, fingering the embossed leather neckband. "Very sexy—what does it say...?"

She waited for him to read it, but he said nothing, just smiled at her while teasing her nipples by stroking under the edge of her bra. She arched into him only to have him shift backward. Intentionally denying what she wanted. Taking control, making the ache for his mouth on her nipples that much stronger.

"You know what it says."

"Tell me anyway."

With her heart now in her throat, she could barely whisper. "I'm yours."

"I love it when you say that."

Exactly why she'd chosen those words.

The hook at her back popped open. Travis's nails raked her skin as he dragged the straps from her shoulders.

Goose bumps popped up all over. He pulled the see-through cups from her sensitized breasts extra slowly, making her squirm on the spot. Finally, his lips grazed the peaks. He moved from one to the other, pushing her past needy to desperate.

"Please..."

He rewarded her good manners by taking one hard bud between his teeth. She moaned at the sharp zing of pleasure that shot straight between her legs. His hot, wet mouth closed over her breast, suckling while his teeth continued their delicious assault.

"Touch me, Travis, make me come."

A growl vibrated against her breast. He released her nipple, scooped her up as if she were light as air, and headed for the bedroom. He had her on her back and both of them divested of clothes before she could catch her breath.

He moved with grace, stealth and the power of a jungle cat. "I've been thinking about this all week." His shoulders pushed her thighs apart. "About you, naked and open for me, like this. The way you taste when I bury my face between your legs." And that's what he did. Covered her with his mouth, dipped inside her with his tongue, sucked her clit between his lips. "I could lick you every day and it wouldn't be enough."

"You won't get an argument from me on that."

"I have six days to make up for—guess we won't be leaving this room for a while." His head dipped again until all she could see were his eyes, dark with desire and focused on her face. He loved watching her come, he'd told her, though for all the times he'd brought her to climax, she'd never been able to keep her eyes open and look into his.

Maybe this time.

He licked her with long, flat swipes before centering his attention on her clit. He danced circles around it. Teased it with hints of vibration, humming in satisfaction when she thrust her hips upward in a physical plea for more.

She wiggled as his fingers entered her. More, deeper, that's what she needed. He pushed farther, easing in and out of her while flicking her clit with his tongue. So good—so very, very good. His pinky joined in, nestling against her ass, breaching her ever so slightly with each thrust.

"Oh god, that, yes..." She clutched his head, writhing and moaning through the stars and bright light. "Shit."

His head jerked up. "Have I lost my touch after a week away?"

"Your touch is perfect as ever. It's just—I closed my eyes. Again." She felt him smile against her thigh. Saw it in his eyes.

"You always close your eyes. It's one of the ways I know I'm hitting the right notes. You're my sexy angel when you close your eyes and come. So beautiful." He licked her sensitive flesh one more time and started to crawl up, over her body, pausing when his eyes snagged on her newly tattooed hip. "It's like mine."

"Yes and no." Calli held her breath while he examined it. She'd had Travis's tattoo artist modify a section of one of her favorites. Travis's forearm had an exquisite dove trapped in a tangle of thorny vines—she'd traced the scene a hundred times, had it committed to memory. Travis had drawn it, and though he'd shrugged it off as *just a sketch* when she asked him about it originally, she knew its meaning as well as he did. In her tattoo, the dove was free, perched atop those vines with a red rose in its beak.

That she got him so completely, had done this for him, hit him deep. He kissed the ink first, working his way up until he covered her with his body.

"Are you upset... about the tattoo?"

One day she'd stop worrying. She'd wake up and realize that *he* was the lucky one, not the other way around. If it took him the rest of their lives, he'd keep showing her.

He cupped her face in his hands. "I love it. I love you." Then he slid home, skin-to-skin inside the sweet embrace of her body, the way it should be, and had been, since they'd officially moved in together. Permanent. Committed. Something he'd never experienced until Calli.

"I missed you," she whispered.

"I almost drove home every night, in the middle of the night, just to lie next to you, even for a couple of hours."

She yanked his head down, kissed him as if her life depended on it. Yeah, he knew that feeling.

He curled his hand under her ass, tilting her hips forward. His balls snugged-up under his cock. No amount of jerking off made the ache go away. He needed to fuck *her*. Craved it. *Her* pussy, so tight and perfect around his cock. Made for him. He couldn't remember any woman before her—couldn't imagine ever wanting anybody else.

Her legs folded around his back as he plunged inside again. She made that sound, that soft little half-frustrated moan that told him she wanted to come but couldn't quite get there. He'd bet she wasn't aware of the tell-tale slip. A secret he planned to keep, since it put him a position to be her hero, over and over again.

He rolled, pulling her on top. He hitched her left leg high on his hip and maneuvered her right leg between his thighs. She gasped when he thrust, eyes wide and mouth open.

"You like?" he asked, guiding her down to meet his next stroke, urging her to grind against him as he filled her, balls-deep.

"Yes, that's so... just do it again."

Didn't have to tell him twice. He thrust again and again, matching the rhythm she needed. Fighting the building pressure at the base of his cock.

He watched her mouth open, her bottom lip catch between her teeth. The dreamy glaze of her eyes as they fluttered half-closed. Her breathing went shallow and her muscles clenched around his cock. And that other sound she made, the louder, lower one as she started to come, filled his head.

"Oh fuck, can't wait..." he rasped as he lost it, and himself, inside the woman he loved.

He could've stayed that way—Calli plastered atop his body—all night, if not for something digging into his back. He fished around the bed and came up with the culprit. The ring. She'd removed it in the living room, now here it was, still off her hand, carving a notch in his shoulder blade. Time to rectify things.

He flipped them again. She went willingly, as she always did for him, but twice as readily when she was dopey on orgasm-induced endorphins. Long dark hair fanned over the pale duvet. Lips rosy from kissing. Two deep-pink nipples topping two perfect tits. The curve of her waist and hips, the sweet vee between her legs that tempted him even now, minutes after coming. And the tattoo. Fucking phenomenal.

"You're staring."

"Admiring what's mine, according to the collar, anyway." He held up the ring. "Not according to this, though."

"I'm sorry." She reached for it and failed, her hand trailing slowly down his chest instead. "Ask me again?"

"Touch me like that and I'll give you anything you want." Hell, he'd give her anything and everything, 24/7. She had to know that. He caught her left hand. Hesitated. Slid it on her ring finger. "Fuck tradition and diamonds and money in the bank. Marry me now."

"I don't need any of those things, only you."

He lowered himself to his elbows, connecting as much of their bodies as possible. His smile stretched so wide across his face, it hurt. "So that's a yes?"

"Bingo."

Thank You!

Thank you for reading **More Than Words**!

I hope you enjoyed Travis and Calli's dirty-Scrabble love story as much as I loved writing it! If so, I would greatly appreciate you spreading the word, including leaving a review or star-rating at your favorite online retailer, or wherever you enjoy discussing books. Again, thanks for reading!

Sincerely,

Karla Doyle

ABOUT THE AUTHOR

Karla is a small town girl with some big city experience, happiest living somewhere in between. She studied fashion design in college and spent most of her adult life in that industry. These days, she lives a charmed existence with her two amazing kids, an incredible (and smokin' hot) husband, and the best friends in the world. When she's not writing the sexy stories that swirl around in her head, you can find her lifting weights at the gym, playing Scrabble, or cuddled up with a book, surrounded by a pack of pets.

Visit Karla's website

for a complete booklist and other information:

www.karladoyle.com

Connect with Karla Online:

www.facebook.com/KarlaDoyleAuthor

www.instagram.com/KarlaDoyleAuthor

www.pinterest.com/KarlaDoyleStuff

www.twitter.com/Karla_Doyle

Send Karla an email:

karla@karladoyle.com

More Books by Karla Doyle

Gift Wrapped

After catching her boyfriend cheating the week before Christmas, Brinn is seriously lacking in holiday spirit. So when she looks into the eyes of a last-minute shopper after closing on Christmas Eve, she's sarcastic rather than sympathetic. But Brinn is ever the good girl and her conscience wins out. She offers the handsome stranger ten minutes to select a gift and ends up with a present of her own—a date. On Christmas Eve.

Davis hates Christmas. Especially this year, since a neighborhood heist liberated him of his hard-earned belongings and the few gifts he'd purchased. But the robbery led him to a cute store manager with a sense of humor, smokin' body and no plans for the evening. Mistletoe might be in order after all.

Their Christmas Eve date is like gift-wrapped, sexy satisfaction. But the best gifts keep on giving, and one naughty night may not be enough—for either of them.

Cup of Sugar (Close to Home #1)

Nia has one rule—don't date neighbors. Simple, except the guy next door is single, handsome, and not inclined to close his blinds while naked. When her car dies, Conn takes "being neighborly" to a new level by offering a ride to her long-distance destination. Nia has resisted his looks and charm for months. Surely she can handle a few hours in his truck...

For months, Conn has blatantly put himself on display, hoping his pretty blonde neighbor would tire of secretly watching and come knock on his door for a cup of sugar—or more. No such luck—until an unusual opportunity arises. After a six-hour drive turns into a sweet-and-sexy weekend, Conn wants more than neighborly status with Nia. To get it, he must convince her to break the rule protecting her heart—by putting his on the line.

Icing on the Cake (Close to Home #2)

Nia and Conn's wedding will be fairytale perfect...if their siblings can get along.

Free-spirited, anti-establishment Sara has always been on the outside of her family's fairytale mold. Now she's being forced smack into the middle of it at her sister Nia's wedding. Alongside the cocky and annoyingly sexy best man—Conn's cop brother.

Curtis doesn't buy in to organized romance and fairytales. But for his brother, he'll throw on a tux and fake it for a few hours. His flak vest would have been a better choice around the maid of honor. He should have brought his handcuffs too, because somebody needs to restrain the dark-haired spitfire—and he's just the man for the job.

One night to indulge the spark between them, then goodbye— that was the agreement. Curtis isn't looking for a relationship and he sure doesn't want a troublemaker for a girlfriend. The last thing Sara needs in her daily life is a cop looking over her shoulder, no matter how hot he is.

But giving in to their chemistry is much more fun than giving it up...

Crossing the Line

Lifelong best friends Derrick and Jeremy met Hanna at a bar ten years ago. Both wanted her—one married her. Now the other man has been invited to join in for one hot weekend.

Everything would've been fine if they'd had their fun that weekend, then gone back to normal. But they didn't. And when past demons resurface, things will never be the same—for any of them.

Body of Work

Cassie has fantasized about the ginger-haired personal trainer for months. Brian is friendly, but never more—until he appears on her doorstep and shows her how much her flirting has affected him. The more she's with him, the more Cassie wants the fairytale, not just hot sex with the six-two hunk. She can give Brian full access to her body, but after her ex's reaction to her explicit photography business, sharing her secrets, and her heart, isn't an option.

Brian knows better than to break the rules. Don't date gym members. Keep his inner beast on a leash during sex. Cassie tested his resolve on number one her first day in the gym. Shattered the second rule when he touched her. The petite pixie shares his preferences in the bedroom. She makes him laugh and love—but past mistakes haunt him, emotionally and tangibly. Cassie's worth the price he'll pay for breaking the rules. Now he must convince her to give him her heart.

Game Plan

Recently divorced after seventeen years with a snooty, uptight, controlling man, forty-year-old Andie is definitely ready for some casual, sexy fun when a hot younger man "accidentally" hits her with a baseball. Mason's interest is clear and he looks like a lot more fun than her overworked vibrator collection, so she goes for it, despite the obvious age gap. The young veterinarian is as easy to be with as he is on the eyes, making him an ideal summer diversion and the perfect man to help her make up for lost time and missed orgasms.

Mason had to meet the sexy woman at the ball diamond. The chemistry between them is instant and completely addictive. Andie is more than beautiful, she's uninhibited and independent—totally unlike the needy twenty-somethings he's been dating since his ex-fiancée deceived him five years ago. And yeah, Andie is ten years older than him, big deal. The more they're together, the more his heart wants her as badly as his cock. Too bad Andie isn't playing for keeps.

Stealing Home

When Paige's latest attempt at happily-ever-after with a nice guy tanks, she decides to quit fighting her destiny. She craves bad boys. Men who deliver short-term, panty-melting excitement, not reliability and settling down. If she's going to embrace her true nature, who better to start with than the dark-haired, tattooed ballplayer whose cocky attitude gives her more thrills than any steady boyfriend ever has...

Alex had major league plans for his life until it threw him an unexpected and unwelcome curve ball. Switching gears to pursue his other passion was a rough road, but things are good—aside from his MIA muse. When a chance meeting with a blonde firecracker stirs his creative juices—and more—Alex is game to see where their chemistry leads. Trouble is, his potential Miss Right thinks she's only capable of playing the field.

Visit **www.karladoyle.com** for a complete list of available and upcoming titles.